Breeds

W. Tussinger

PublishAmerica
Baltimore

First printing

ISBN: 1-4137-8701-0
PUBLISHED BY PUBLISHAMERICA, LLLP
www.publishamerica.com
Baltimore

Printed in the United States of America

To my good friend
Lewis A. Williamson

"The Clothes Line"

For grandmother long since promoted to heaven.

I love standing in the sunshine feeling the breeze,
Smelling the freshness of clean clothes hanging on the line.
It brings back memories of laughter and running
My arms waving in the winds
Like the clothes on the line.
Little toes grabbing the ground
Like the clothespins pinching my socks.
Grandmother washed clothes in the yard
Using a tub and washboard.
She wore an apron that slipped over her head
Over her chest.
It tied in the back holding her together
Like the basket holding our clothes.
Her short black hair was held back
With bobby pins yet tendrils fell
Over her face of crinkley brown leaves
And would flutter around her eyes
Like the arms of my long-sleeved shirts
When they flapped in the wind
Her smile was like the sunshine and she loved me.

Chapter 1

Hello, my name is Willa Mae Twosinger. Like both my parents, I'm a half-breed. Because Wyandotte Indians are matriarchal and my momma had a clan, I got one. That would be mud turtle.

This here's an attempt to put down on paper some of the events of my upbringing. I started life in rural Oklahoma, Indian Territory, as it was first named. To some extent it was Indian Territory, but not wholeheartedly.

The time frame was post-depression, pre-getting over it. I wouldn't say we was poor, though. It seems to me that "poor" is as much a mindset as a financial status. In the first sense we were holdin' our own, in the second sense, well, let's just say there were colors we seen more often than green.

Poppa was a horse trader of sorts, all kinda sorts. What we didn't have in cash he tried to make up for in "stuff." Tradin' was more a way of life back then than now. Just about any transaction could take place without anyone ever reaching into their pockets.

Momma and Poppa were both half Indian and half Scotch-Irish. That's where I got the title to this here book, because back then, being a half-breed wasn't always the easiest thing in the world. Other Indians, "full bloods," looked at half-breeds in a half let down, half-disgusted way. Like, somehow, anyone that would be born only half Indian was a traitor to "Indian-ness." Whites just looked on us in disgust.

If someone really wanted to hurt someone's feelings, there were two phrases that always seemed to leap to the offenders tongue, one was "breed"; the other one referred to our Negro counterparts.

Perhaps in my psyche I think that to take this word and make it "my" word in this literary effort I'm somehow taking the power to hurt me with it out of the hands of those that used to hurl it at me. Much in the same way the other word has been claimed by those it used to be used against.

But this story ain't a "I been wronged" treatise. It's just a story of how I grew up. And overall, I'd have to say I had a pretty good upbringing.

Chapter 2

"Willa Mae, you get them potatoes out here now, girl." It was Momma, calling from the dining room.

I hurriedly turned off the propane stove in the kitchen, and using a rag as a potholder, carried the frying pan heaped with cut potatoes into the dining room where the family was waiting for them at the table. There was Poppa, Momma, my two older brothers, one younger brother and Uncle Bear.

Uncle Bear, Bear was his last name, had come calling earlier in the day. He was "just out visitin" he said. Of course, this entitled him to one free meal, Momma insisted, and he didn't put up much of a fight resistin'. Come to think of it I don't even think he was a true uncle to us. But he was family somehow, if not blood then kindred, as Poppa would say.

Everybody liked Uncle Bear. He was a truly friendly type. Bald as a beet on top, he still had hair on the sides. I've heard some say Indians don't go bald, that's a romantic stereotype, but it ain't so. Uncle Bear loved to laugh, and he'd always slap one knee or the other with the palms of his hands.

As I set the skillet down on the table, I glanced at Uncle Bear, who gave me a curious wink. No sooner had I set down the potatoes than spoons were reaching for them, plates being filled. Potatoes, green beans with bacon, pork chops and homemade Indian tortilla bread was what we was havin'.

As soon as his plate was sufficiently stacked, Uncle Bear started talking. He was a wide traveler, just started up his old Cadillac and went wherever he got the notion. He was talking about his latest trip to Mexico.

"And, Sue Ann," that was Momma's real name, "you believe what I ate while I was down Mexico way?" He took a pause here while the air of impatience had time to build sufficiently. "Rocky Mountain oysters!" he blurted out, like a jokester giving out the punch line of a joke.

The boys all started laughing. Silas, my little brother, just because he wanted to feel he was a part of the club. Momma blushed, and from the look she gave me, I held my tongue from asking the obvious question, "What are those?" Del, my eldest brother, asked, "Were those with or without the handle?" This must have been even funnier by the laughter it evoked, and the shade of blush Momma took on from it.

Then Momma gave "the look" and Poppa spoke up quickly, "All right, that's enough, not at the table," while still trying to gain a straight face.

Uncle Bear took the initiative and chimed in, "Oh, that reminds me, I just happen to have run across a little something." With that said he reached under the table and produced a package wrapped in newspaper with Spanish writing all over it. This he handed to me.

The sheer exoticness of the wrapping took my breath away. I'd never seen writing other than English, the fact that it was nothing more than disposed of newspaper didn't matter one bit. Until Momma and Poppa both prompted me to open it in unison the thought that there was more under the paper never even occurred to me.

But when it did I tore the package open like the yesterdays' headlines that they were. There, on my lap sitting at the table was as pretty a dress as I'd ever laid eyes on.

"It ain't exactly like our own Native dress that the old folks used to wear, after the leather dresses, of course, but it's close," Uncle Bear was saying. "I picked it up down Sonora way from an Indian down that-a-way."

I was standing, holding the dress up to myself, picturing myself in it. Momma was saying how beautiful it was and Poppa was nodding his approval. It was a full-length dress, and the skirt part, from the hip down, had three layers of cloth to it, making it fuller.

"Heah! How come you got her something extra like that. Uncle Bear?" blurted out Silas.

"Well now, Silas," started Uncle Bear in a conciliatory tone, "Willa Mae's becoming a young woman now. Women folk, they need that sorta thing."

"A woman? Willa Mae? Yeah right, and I'm a fox that don't eat chickens!"

Poppa's glare just caught him before he started into another analogy intended to illustrate his disbelief.

"Eat ya' supper first, girl, then you can go upstairs and try it on," Momma said.

As I sat back down, having carefully placed the dress safely out of harm's way from any table accidents on a bureau nearby, I eyed Silas stroking his extended index finger on one hand with his index finger of the other hand in my direction. A definitive "shame-shame on you" gesture.

"Now you stop that, Silas Ray," cautioned Momma.

"I almost had to drop one of them Lovett boys today," spoke up Del. "Damn, if I didn't come out of the general store and there the three were. Jerrad he says, 'Hey look, the breed.' He started to say more but I steps right up to him and looked him in the eye. I'd a hit him, but Sheriff Mills just happened to be there and he was quick to make his presence known. I didn't waste no more time on him then, I just went my way."

Del was the eldest, nigh twenty-two years old. He was big and had dark hair and skin. He could surely handle himself, too, if things got fightin' serious. Both Del and the brother betwixt us, Walt, were tall, stout, boys. They looked Indian all right. Me, I was light skinned with light brown hair and brownish-green eyes, and nobody couldn't hardly tell I was even Indian, till they knew what family I was from. Silas, he was a mix, tanned skin color but dark hair and eyes.

"Don't you place too much stock in that Sheriff Mills neither," Poppa cautioned.

"He just does his job," Momma interjected quickly. I knew this was Momma's way of trying to change the subject.

"Problem is with 'just doing one's job,'" Poppa pressed on, "is the false assumption that a man can separate what he gets paid to do with what he is as a person."

After that there was a long moment of silence at the table. I'd only heard parts of the story but I knew that, before I was born, Sheriff Mills had come to force Momma and Poppa to give up Del to go to an "Indian school" out in Washington State somewhere.

That was the practice back then and still was. Indian kids from there were brought here and kids from here were tooken there. Momma said it was because the government wanted to brainwash us kids and so had to keep us as far away from our blood as possible. Anyway, Daddy resisted and went to jail for a while, but Del never got took. None of us kids after that were ever sent for again.

It was Uncle Bear who broke the silence. "Well?" We were all looking at him expecting more. "Am I going to get to see my niece in the dress I gave her from plump down Mexico way or not?"

Before I could be prompted further, I was out of my chair and running up the stairs, dress in hand.

Chapter 3

Momma and Poppa were in their room with the door closed. As I'd done many times before, I was crouched down on all fours listening intently outside the door. They were speaking in the Wyandotte Indian language to each other.

We children were never allowed to hear the language. But when they were alone, my parents often reverted back to their first language. Our family came from a long line of half-breeds. Both of my grandparent sets were half-breeds as well. I don't know before that exactly, but somewhere back there, there was a pure blood Wyandotte and a non-Indian on each side.

It's been explained to me that originally the Indian folk didn't have a name for a half-breed. Either you were or you weren't, and color wasn't the deciding factor neither, it was how you lived. Any non-Wyandotte could be accepted into the tribe as a full member, as if he'd been born a member, no distinctions.

That person would have to live like a Wyandotte is all. Back in those days that must have been a lot though. They'd have to learn the language, customs and all. One story Uncle Bear once told me was of a white boy the Wyandottes found abandoned in a wash. He was just a toddler and when they found him he was so hungry he was eating the mud in the wash. That boy grew up to be a great chief among the people, Chief Mudeater.

Momma says it's because of this custom that our tribe had so much variety in our skin colors, from dark to light as me. Poppa says, "The percentages given to people like half-breed, quarter-breed and so on was all the devil-government's doing." That's how he always referred to the government. "Real people don't divide themselves up. Only a damn fool..." Well, Poppa got pretty mad usually by this time just talking about it so Momma would step in before he really got to cussing. We'd either be sent to bed or the subject would be changed, quick.

Anyhow, we kids were told we were better off not to learn the Wyandotte language. "It's a changing world, and our language ain't got no part in it," they'd say. "You'll just be hampered, knowing two languages, concentrate on one and you'll be better off."

I was suddenly startled by a familiar voice behind me, "Tsk, tsk, I'm a gonna tell Mom." It was my brat little brother Silas.

With that I was off, "Like a thoroughbred in a horse race," Poppa would have said. Silas ran past me toward his room as I made a grab for him, missing. Silas knew that if he made it to his room that I wouldn't pursue him any farther, I let him clear the threshold then skipped into my room across the hall.

I hadn't really been interested in extracting any physical revenge on Silas, I was just playing along, plus I wanted out of the hall before Momma or Poppa came to their door. I had heard a few new words that I could remember. Momma and Poppa had been talking shopping list so I assumed that the words were staples around the house. I'd repeat them over and over to myself to remember them then use them in a sentence to Uncle Bear. He wouldn't teach me any Wyandotte either, knowing how Momma and Poppa felt, but he'd correct me if I used the words; that's how I found their meaning usually.

It wasn't long and Momma was calling me to come help cook breakfast. Cooking was a woman's chore Momma always said. "And eatin's a man's," I said back. I complained about always doing the dishes but I knew when it came time to haul wood or do hard outside work I'd get to stay inside while the boys were called upon by Poppa to help.

Sometimes, if'n Silas whined or didn't pull his weight a helpin' outside, he'd be made to help me do the dishes. I made it so miserable for him on these instances that he was usually eager to work outside the next day. I'd call him "sis" and tell him he was a real princess for helping me. On a good day I could even make him cry.

Today we kids were all going over to Uncle Bear's place. He lived about five miles away. It was a nice warm day outside and it would be a good walk. After breakfast I rushed to get the dishes done. The boys finished their chores outside in record time and we were off.

There was me, Silas, Walt and Del. My two older brothers each had a .22 rifle thrown over their shoulders. They rarely went anywhere without them except to town. Uncle Bear lived near the crick in a rock house he'd built himself.

All us kids enjoyed going to Uncle Bear's. We always had fun there. There was an old barn on the premises. It was real old and decrepit. It had been there before Uncle Bear had built his place and it was off limits to us kids.

Uncle Bear told us there were only two rules at his place: have fun and be safe. It fell under the second rule that we weren't to go near this old barn. So, of course, that's where we'd planned on going today.

Silas, he was chunkin' rocks with his bean flip, also called a slingshot, as we walked the dirt road. We had to stop once to let a mother skunk and her four little ones go by. We knowed better than to mess with them and kept our distance.

In no time flat we reached Uncle Bear's place. Once there we were warmly greeted by Uncle Bear who always seemed genuinely glad to have us visit. Silas told him some little story, and as usual Uncle Bear laughed out loud and slapped his bald head like he was tickled pink to hear such a funny story. None of us thought the story was funny but nonetheless Silas was bursting with pride.

We was offered soda-pop, which we took thirstily, and quickly excused ourselves. Me and Silas raced out the door. Del and Walt retreated with a little more dignity. The last words I heard as I turned the corner of the house was Uncle Bear's usual admonition to "have fun but be safe."

The four of us headed down toward the crick bed. Silas caught a big toad and goaded me with it while I screamed at him to stop. Del and Walt took some practice shots at tree trunks. A large snapping turtle slid back into the water as we ambled in the direction of the old barn.

Chapter 4

The day had turned out to be a beautiful one, warm, with an occasional light wind that refreshed. I was wearing the dress that Uncle Bear had given me. I'd been eager to show him how much I adored it. Because of that I was gingerly making my way along as the boys moved on ahead of me.

As I topped off on the edge of the bank, I could hear my two older brothers shooting their guns and the excited squeals of Silas as they obviously had found a target. I picked up my pace as I reached level ground and did a skip-run towards the old barn.

The barn was made of old cracked boards nailed on a rustic frame. There were double doors, and one always hung half open and half off its hinges. The top hinge on this door had long since broken in half. It had matched the other hinges, worn rubber, all cut from old tires and nailed to door and frame. There were ample cracks and spaces in the feeble walls to let light into the structure.

It was from this setting that I could hear the shouts of enthusiasm and rifle shots emitting. Edging myself through the half hanging, half open door, carefully, lest I snag my dress on anything, I entered to see Del and Walt taking aim at several large rats on the opposite side of the structure. Silas, too, was reloading his bean flip with a rock for his chance.

As soon as Del and Walt fired in unison, one rat disappeared under the plank flooring while one more joined the injured list, running in place and seemingly trying to bite at the unseen enemy that burned itself into its flesh. There was also one more that littered the barn floor that wouldn't be moving again.

"Ooo..." I screamed as I saw what was causing such excitement in my brothers. These were large rats, almost as big as small cats. As my eyes adjusted to the semi-gloom, I could see many more rising out of the battered floor planking to see what was threatening their nest of many years. Looking down I could see the ground just a foot or so below the widely spaced wood flooring.

I thought I could see holes dug in the earth, and movement. Screaming again I headed for three old bales of straw stacked off to the side, two on the floor and one on top so a chair was formed.

"There's rats under the floor," I squealed.

"Well now, that's an original thought. You figure that out all by your lonesome or did you have to have Silas here help you out?" smarted Walt.

"Yeah, you figure that out all by your lonesome?" copied Silas.

"No really, the whole ground is moving under the flooring," I insisted.

Bending over to catch a better glimpse, Del tried to peer through the old planking. The boys were slightly under the loft several feet above their heads and so were in the shadows more than from where I stood atop the second bale of straw. Even though the dilapidated roof let a lot of light in, it was still a shadowy place under the far-reaching loft.

"Silas," Del shouted, "go get that old lantern over yonder."

Silas rushed over to where Del had pointed. There were several old tools still strewn throughout the barn and one old lantern hanging on a rusty nail. Retrieving this, Silas carried it back to Del. Del carried matches with him and quickly had the kerosene lamp lit. It didn't have much kerosene in it but it had enough to light and last for a little while at least.

Peering down through the plank floor cracks my three brothers could now see what looked like hundreds, or even thousands, of scurrying forms just below their feet.

"Ooo...wow!" exclaimed Silas.

Walt quickly started to reload his rifle. It was Del who first started to perceive the full implications of what they'd gotten themselves into. Silas, in his excitement to get a rock out of his pocket full to reload his bean flip, ran towards me and placed the lantern he'd been holding on the first bale of straw below me.

The next sound I heard was the crack of Walt's .22 as he felled another large rat that was just climbing up through the flooring.

"That's enough!" shouted Del.

"What's the matter?" asked Walt with surprise, turning to catch an odd expression on his older brother's face. Following Del's stare we all looked in disbelief as the floor planking of the old barn came alive with scurrying, long, thick-tailed rats. As they approached my brothers and the straw bale I was on, I screamed in true terror. There were hundreds of rats, and they were on the offensive.

I saw Del fire the single shot he had in the barrel of his gun and take his rifle by the barrel to use as a club. Silas out screamed me, and then Walt picked him up by one arm and the seat of his pants and chucked him my way like a bag of potatoes. He landed sprawled on the first bale of hay at my feet, knocking the lantern over onto the plank floor and breaking it.

One rat, on fire from the broken kerosene lamp, leaped onto the bale of straw where Silas had landed just as I helped pull him up to my bale. Glancing over toward my other two brothers I saw them swinging their rifles in every direction as rats scurried angrily at their feet.

In that brief instant of time, a scene that's been etched into my memory ever since, I saw Del clubbing a rat in mid air just as it had dropped from the loft above. I saw Walt throw his rifle sideways at a trio of attacking rats on the ground as he made a desperate leap for a nearby shovel leaning against a log loft support. Then I heard Silas scream, almost in my ear.

Looking down where I thought Silas had fallen at my feet I saw him patting desperately with both hands at the skirt of my dress. Not until then did I realize that half of my dress skirt was in flames. Because of the many layers of the dress skirt, I hadn't felt a thing yet. I screamed in response.

Now, motivated by sheer terror, I took one last look in Del's direction and jumped. I knew the desperation in Del's eyes in that brief instant as he saw my dress on fire and knew he'd not be able to make it to me in time to offer help. They were in a sea of moving teeth and tails now.

Jumping over rats, I flew out the cocked doorway into the bright outside. As I threw myself into the grass, I was almost instantly being rolled by Uncle Bear, who magically appeared out of nowhere. I heard my father calling for my brothers as he must have been heading into the barn. Then I heard my mother's scream as she caught up to the scene from the bank of the stream we'd so recently ascended.

Once I was out, the skirt torn from my dress completely in order to quench the fire, Uncle Bear headed into the barn himself. Seconds later Poppa tore out the barn door opening holding Silas in his arms. I could see the shock in Silas' face as he was laid down on the grass beside me and Momma. Then Poppa started to rise to return to the barn just as Uncle Bear, Del and Walt poured into the outside yard.

The blaze started in the barn by the broken lamp was visible through the barn wall cracks now. Growing quickly, it was spreading throughout the old structure, aided by the layers of dried straw and hay from years past. There were also the sounds of screeching rats as they chose to retreat to their holes just below the plank flooring only to be cooked in their burrows by the now all-consuming blaze.

Looking over at the whimpering Silas, I saw he still held much of my burnt skirt in his hands. Then I realized as Momma and Poppa tried to remove it that the material had actually melted onto his hands. At a safe distance from the engulfed barn, Poppa gingerly peeled away the layers of material while Uncle Bear took Del and Walt off to the side, just out of sight, and made them strip completely so he could find out if they'd been bit or not.

As the old barn burned and crumpled to the ground in the background, the entire family was soon all huddled around Silas. Silas' head resting on Momma's lap, Poppa continued to peel away at the layers of material. Me and Momma cried freely but there were no dry eyes in that crowd. Silas seemed the calmest one there, in fact. Though he whimpered, he never bawled.

After several minutes the layers were removed to reveal the charred remains of Silas' hands. Gently Poppa reached over and picked Silas up. Del had stepped up to get Silas, but Poppa shook his head; no one would carry his son in this hour of need but Poppa. Del understood as we all did.

Chapter 5

In the week that had passed, Silas' burns were slowly healin'. Thanks to Uncle Bear's herbs, there were no signs of infection. Uncle Bear was considered to be a medicine man by many folk in our parts, although he never claimed that title for himself. He had Silas on a strict regimen of oral herb concoctions and salve that was changed once a day on Silas' hands.

Del and Walt weren't hurt too seriously. They each had bites and scrapes but there were no signs or symptoms of rabies or any other such diseases. Uncle Bear had them on their own regimens of herbs, spices and salves. The barn no longer existed and any rats that survived the inferno were dispersed.

On the day after the incident, Poppa had gotten so desperate he had even let Momma take Silas to the local Indian Health Clinic. He really didn't trust anything government run.

And he had good reason for that. We knew one Indian lady who'd been told to douche with Clorox water to treat a female problem by the local Indian Health Service doctor. She was never able to have children after that. The doc had just told Momma that if Silas lived at all, his hands would just be worthless clubs and his fingers would grow together as they were burned so badly.

Looking back, I believe Poppa's mistrust of the government

hospital was well founded. Besides all the poor medical advice, it was common practice for the dentists, which came out once a month, to simply remove teeth rather than to treat them, on the Indians at least. I guess they didn't want to take the time to fill teeth so they just yanked them out. It was common in those days for the Indians around where I grew up to be totally toothless by the time they were twenty years old. Sometimes they were given false teeth, sometimes not.

I'd never heard Momma cuss before that day. She'd stormed out of the doctor's office and slammed the door behind her. She didn't cuss directly at the doctor but, boy, did she let his memory have a tongue lashin' on the way home. Poppa was furious when she told him what the doctor had said, right in front of Silas himself. Since then Uncle Bear was Silas' doctor.

There was one hope of quick and complete healing that momma was determined to try, Brother Terran was coming to our neck of the woods. Poppa, Del and Walt teased momma about believing in such "white witchcraft" as Poppa called it. They took to calling Brother Terran "brother terror."

Brother Terran was a traveling tent revival preacher of fire and brimstone proportions. Once a year he breezed through, preached all night sometimes, often taking five or six offerings during the course of a single meeting. He was fond of starting out his meeting with, "Leave your watches at home folks, because you've just entered Gods' time zone," I guess to emphasize that he'd often invite people to place their time pieces in the offering plates.

That night was to be his opening night. Momma and me rushed to get ready just as soon as supper was eaten and the chores were completed.

Silas had to be dressed and cared for now. Poppa fed Silas in the evening when he was back from work and me and momma took turns during the day. Since the accident, Poppa had become more morose. He tried to hide it but there was a bitterness to his conversation now. Before, he tended to be open-minded, always striving to see the other side of every argument. Now he just took his side and the other side be dammed.

Soon we were loading Silas into our pick-up truck. Me and Momma piled in while Walt hopped behind the wheel to drive us. Momma didn't drive and Poppa and Del didn't want to go anywhere near Brother Terran.

The tent was located in a big open field, not far from home. We piled out of the truck and found some empty seats under the tent top. Brother Terran's revivals were considered to be top notch. He had chairs and a raised platform, all that he carried with him from place to place. Up toward the front, in front of the raised platform where he'd preach his sermon, there was an area marked by sawdust thrown down that marked what he called his "holy of holies" area. To even step in this area one had to remove their shoes.

Many of the faithful would just kick off their shoes right from the get-go in anticipation of going forward when invited. When we arrived there was already hymns being sung. The song leader, a big fat woman with jowls that vibrated as she urged us to show our faith with our upraised voices, was exhorting participation. Ushers, chosen from the local faithful, were located around the holy of holies area to chastise any errant kids, or adults, who would stray onto the cordoned section with shoes on.

We sang along as best we could, not really being familiar with all the songs. The seats filled up, leaving standing room only. Hours passed as we sang and re-sang hymns. We were told that Brother Terran was "wrestling with the very forces of the devil for our poor miserable souls" in prayer. Due to the abundance of wickedness in our area, he was praying through, believing, till he knew he'd overcome the dominion of Satan in our lives.

This impressed us greatly. Although there were white people present, the majority of those in attendance were Indians, then Negroes. A good revival was the one time when all races came together in them parts. Finally, an authoritative man made his way into the tent from the direction of where we were told Brother Terran was making his supplications for "us poor heathen's souls" in a smaller side tent.

A hushed reverential silence fell over the tent as he replaced the lady leading songs behind the pulpit.

"You'uns all come here tonight po' seekin' souls," he begun, almost singing and out and out shoutin' the words, as there were no microphones. "Well tonight is yo night-of-salvation! Because the great Brother Terran, nay, the humble Brother Terran, has broken through the very doors of Satan with his tears of supplication to the good Lord Almighty! And with those tears he's wrestled the keys to yo' miserable souls from the grip of Satan hisself!"

"Tonight! Is the night of yo' salvation!" Brother Mickey, as I later learned he was called, spent some time exhorting us after this matter. I could feel my own faith growing as Brother Mickey promised us not only salvation but miraculous healings the like as we'd never heard tell. He gave some examples too, from Brother Terran's last revival a few weeks previous in Arkansas.

He told us about the crippled man who was brought to the meeting in a wheeled chair and left leaping and rejoicing that his name was, from that moment forth, written in the lamb's book of life. He had a half dozen or more such examples. Then he stopped all his prancing around the rug where he'd been going from one end to the other and stood still.

"How many of you'uns here tonight believe in the Lord Jesus Almighty?"

As folks tried to out do one another in their verbal confirmation of "amens," "hallelujahs" and the occasional "praise the Lords," Silas leaned over to me and whispered, "'How many of you'uns here tonight believe?' Them Arkansa'ans sure do talk funny don't they?"

Momma was quick to flash a mean look and shake her head. We knew to hush right-off. We weren't too sure if the Good Lord was as mean as Momma could be at times or not, but if'n he even came close, what with all his power and from his vantage point, he might just smote us in our seats.

Then Brother Mickey held up his arms, outstretched to the Lord-like, and the tent fell silent. The musical instruments stopped too; they'd been playing low background music throughout.

"Yes, Lord, I hear you," Brother Mickey spoke up to the Lord.

Then, turning his attention back to us, "The Lord has said that it's time for the healings to begin." There was a smattering of applause as we all waited in anticipation.

"The Lord has also said that as your faith is, so it shall be unto you. How many of you'uns here tonight believe?"

There was a loud chorus of affirmative "amens" and the like; Momma even joined in and shouted an "amen." Next came a barrage of scripture and exhortations from Brother Mickey to put our faith to the test by giving our material possessions, mostly money. Finishing up with the example of the women who only had two mites but gave it all anyway, the offering baskets were finally passed.

Momma gave a little, as we didn't have much. Then Brother Mickey left the stage with a flourish and we waited. Before too long the music started back up, slow and soft at first then the tempo started to build finally, just as Silas crawled onto the ground to fall asleep, Brother Terran bounded onto the platform. His preaching was rapid and he used his big strong voice to boom out to all comers of the tent without the use of a microphone. I looked around for the first time then and realized that the tent was packed. I'd guess 300 plus people were in attendance, and this was the first night.

What I remember about that first great Pentecostal sermon I'd ever heard was how Brother Terran used our emotions to stimulate us to faith. At one point I remember he stopped in mid-sentence and stood stock-still. Then he looked down at his own two feet. "I just realized, " he stated, "I just realized what big foot prints I'm standing in." We all craned our necks to see what he saw. Then he continued.

"I'm following in the footprints of great faith healers like Elijah, Paul, and Peter. I'm also standing in the footprints of great disciples. Men like Moses, who once prayed the ground open beneath the unbelievers in his congregation and they fell straight into hell with their britches still on."

"Are there any unbelievers here tonight?" he challenged. I was terrified. I thought I could even feel the ground moving beneath my feet. Shortly thereafter another offering was taken, another chance for us to show our faith by giving out of our need so our "cup could runneth over" later.

Momma and me emptied out our pockets this time, as I imagine most everyone present did also. Even Walt gave a dollar.

Still later that night Brother Terran invited people to come up and get prayed for. It was the time for the "laying on of hands." Over half the adults and many of the children, those who were still awake, lined up for this one-on-one prayer time, myself included. As we crowded toward the front "holiest of holies" area we left our shoes behind where we'd been sitting.

Then Brother Terran and his elders started laying hands on each of our foreheads as we made our private supplications to the Lord. Myself, and I'm sure Momma too, asked for Silas' healing. Before we left that night, Brother Terran exhorted us to believe in the healings we'd already received. By his stripes we *were* healed, past tense, he pointed out. But we had to be careful lest the devil steal that seed of faith from our hearts.

Chapter 6

We'd attended two more nights of the revival. By the third night, Poppa wasn't letting me or Momma take any money with us, or even wear any jewelry. Brother Terran believed women shouldn't adorn themselves with such carnal tokens as jewelry. I guess by way of emphasis, last night he'd taken a jewelry offering.

Most of the Indian ladies wore jewelry of one sort or another, and as the offering basket, or in this case it had become a bucket, passed me and Momma by I could see it was nigh unto full. Some ladies were even putting their wedding bands into the bucket to reap the promised ten-fold return on their investment of faith.

Souls were getting added to the kingdom of God Almighty, and Brother Terran even hinted last night that he might extend the camp meeting past the two more nights that were originally planned.

On this bright sunny summer day I was walking toward where Brother Terran's "faith tent" was set up, next to the bigger "all-meetin'" tent. Every night me and Momma had been going up to the "holiest of holies" at the front of the tent. Every night Brother Terran and his disciples had placed their hands of faith on our heads and each time we'd been assured that "by His stripes" Silas *was* already healed.

The difficulty with that is that each morning when Poppa changed Silas' dressings his hands were still the same. I'd talked myself into coming to see Brother Terran in person. Maybe we weren't believing strong enough. Maybe, like Brother Terran often said, we were letting the devil steal Silas' miracle. I didn't understand how the devil could steal something that God had already gave.

These were a few of the thoughts that I had going as I approached Brother Terran's private prayer tent. As I stood at the canvas flap that constituted the entry, I debated with myself as to how to announce my presence. There was nothing to knock on so eventually I just raised my voice.

"Hello, Brother Terran, my name's Willa Mae Twosinger. I've come to ask for a prayer request."

Within seconds Brother Terran was at the flap.

"Well, well, child," Brother Terran greeted me enthusiastically. Just briefly I thought I imagined a slight leer come to his expression as he quickly looked me up and down and then his expression was all fatherly again.

"'Suffer the little ones to come unto me, sayeth the Lord of Hosts," Brother Terran sang. "Come right on in, child."

As I stepped into the tent, Brother Terran straightened the tent flap closed behind me. The insides were a lot more leisurely than I'd expected. Carpet was laid down on the ground and the centerpiece of the tent space was the king-sized bed.

I remember it was a king-sized bed because I'd only heard tell of such a large bed. The tent itself was good sized. I seen some small revivals held in similar sized tents.

"Please, dear child, take a seat on the bed. This is not only my place of prayer and supplication but it also serves as my personal quarters."

As I did as I was directed, I was impressed by the large number of boxes off to one side on the ground. Some seemed to be filled with change, some jewelry, there were even some filled with paper money.

Catching my stare, Brother Terran spoke up, "Just getting all God's chillin's love offerings of faith ready to go out to the po' and afflicted."

Brother Terran looked a little younger than my own father by a few years. He had thick black hair and I thought he looked rather handsome.

"Now, my young lady, tell me, what's on your heart?" said Brother Terran as he sat quite close to me on the edge of the bed.

As I started to tell Brother Terran of Silas' burns and my own personal lack of faith that was keeping him from receiving his God-given healing, I found myself crying profusely. I confessed then how my own guilt, because it was because of my dress catching fire, was why Silas' healing wasn't happening. If only I could believe I knew he'd already have been healed.

Brother Terran was speaking soothing words into my ear. Slowly I felt myself leaning backwards towards the bed. Through my tears and snifflings I suddenly realized that it was actually Brother Terran who was gingerly pulling me backwards. At the same instant I became aware of how close his face was to mine. As if that wasn't enough I suddenly became starkly aware of where Brother Terran's other hand was. I was wearing a soft cotton spring dress. The skirt was just a little below my knees.

At least it had been. Now, however, it was scrunched up considerably higher. Done so by the presence of Brother Terran's left hand that, at present, was resting firmly halfway up my thigh. It was the fact that that hand was still in its upward ascent that snapped me out of my tearful outburst.

Pushing him away I jumped up and ran for the door flap. I remember looking backwards and yelling just before I exited, "I'm a gonna tell my poppa!" Brother Terran uttered some small phrase that sounded something like, "But I just wanted to pray for you."

That evening as Momma headed out for the revival with

Silas, I stayed behind. I never really told Poppa about what had happened with Brother Terran in the tent that day. I lied and told Momma I wasn't feeling too well that evening.

I was afraid of what Poppa would do. Poppa was known to be a pretty docile man generally, but he wasn't to be crossed neither. I knew he carried a gold colored, highly ornate, pistol with him wherever he went. It was small, a derringer, I think they are called. Poppa referred to it as his palmer.

It turned out that Walt, Momma and Silas were back early that evening anyway. Momma explained that Brother Terran had been whisked away by the Lord, kind of like Steven in the Book of Acts. Brother Mickey explained how he saw him interceding for lost souls one instant and in the next he was gone. "Probably found himself ministering to some po' lost soul halfway around the globe."

Anyway, Brother Mickey preached a short sermon and took a long, "silent offering." That was when he didn't want no change, just paper bills. He said it was for some cause or another. Then a quick "blanket prayer" was prayed where him and others just extended their hands over the audience, said a prayer and then dismissed everyone. Silas still wasn't healed.

Chapter 7

The next day me, Del, Walt and Silas were once again headed to Uncle Bear's. The boys were shootin' at squirrels, picking up any if they hit 'em. Poppa always said they had to eat whatever they shot. Walt carried a gunnysack to carry them in. Uncle Bear made the best acorn and squirrel soup you ever could have eaten.

Uncle Bear had never been married. He'd been a military man most of his life. That was a great living for a half-breed in those days, Poppa once told me. I asked Poppa why he hadn't went into the military then. He'd just said, "I met your momma."

By the time we reached Uncle Bear's, Walt had four squirrels in his sack and it was shaping up to be a warm cozy day. Uncle Bear let us know how happy he was to see us, as he always did, and Del and Walt went around back to skin and butcher the squirrels. Uncle Bear was busy cracking acorn seeds, and I started to help. We were outside; on a day like this nobody wanted to be inside.

In Uncle Bear's front yard was a great old tree stump. Sawed flat so as it could be used as a seat, or table, or, as now, as a workbench. Uncle Bear resumed cracking acorn seeds on the stump as Del and Walt disappeared around the back corner of the house. Me and Silas pulled up a wooden bucket, flipped upside down, to sit on.

"Do you believe you're going to hell, Uncle Bear?" Silas popped out first thing.

I hit Silas in the arm, but Uncle Bear didn't seem to mind the question.

"No, no, I don't," stated Uncle Bear thoughtfully. "I reckon I'd have to believe in all of Christianity. The good as well as the bad. Wouldn't be too wise to just believe in the bad part would it?"

Silas was thoughtful for a moment. "Brother Terran said we was all dumb as sheep and needed a shepherd to show us the right from wrong. You're an Indian, how come you don't speak to us in stories like that all the time?"

"You mean comparisons." I elbowed Silas, mostly just for the fun of it.

"Suppose'n I was to use this here old tree stump to make a point," began Uncle Bear after a brief instant of hesitation. "See these rings here? They represent things in your life that you consider important. The closer the ring is to the exact center the closer it is to your heart.

"Say, for instance, this here ring closest to the center is your Momma and Poppa, then Willa Mae here, your brothers and so forth. As you get out here, away from the center, you got your friends, toys, pets, stuff like that."

"But why is the things most important to me the smaller rings?" asked Silas.

"Because they are more dear to you so you guard them closer to your heart," responded Uncle Bear. "Those are the things you take most care for. See, there are a lot of rings here. The trick in life is to know what's really important to you and being able to give or take everything else."

Silas was silent for a long moment as he studied the stump. "But how come these rings on the outside are thicker than the inner rings?"

"That's because this here old tree had better years these last

few years of its life than when it first started growing,"
responded Uncle Bear. "The thicker the ring, the more it
received nourishment and grew that year."

"But how does that relate in your comparison?" asked Silas
earnestly.

Now Uncle Bear was silent for a while. "Well, I guess it don't.
And maybe that's the better lesson, you ain't no tree. You ain't
no sheep neither. Just because something is said in flowery talk
don't make it true. Now pick that there bucket of cracked acorns
up, and let's get lunch on."

With that the lesson was over. I remember other things that
Uncle Bear said that really stuck with me. Things like we
shouldn't throw our fish bones in the fire after we eat the meat.
Uncle Bear said this was disrespectful to the memory of the fish.

Uncle Bear often spoke of harmony between man and
animals and nature. He often told us if we disrespected Mother
Earth, we'd pay for it when we got old. He believed certain
illnesses such as cancers and arthritis were a result of youthful
disrespect of animals and plants and Mother Earth in general.

Often, when he was called upon by local neighbors to help in
a healing way, I'd go along with him and I'd hear his advise
along these lines. There was no penitence involved, just Uncle
Bear's belief that if the patient could recognize where they erred,
maybe they could somehow make peace between themselves
and those they had wronged, be they animal, plant or man.
More often than not the one they'd erred most against was
themselves, Uncle Bear often said.

Chapter 8

That morning started out like any other of recent. Poppa was doing Silas' dressing change. Silas was crying but not more than any other dressing change he'd had in the last two or so weeks since the accident. Poppa was taking great care to separate each and every finger, and his thumbs, from each other and applying Uncle Bear's salve.

The doc up at the Indian Health Service had emphatically said Silas' hands would just be clubs after they healed. Poppa was taking great care so that every digit stayed independent and didn't grow into the next or into the hand itself. Poppa would force each finger to straighten out, against the resistance of his badly damaged muscles. This was when Silas cried the most.

While Poppa did this Momma and me got ready. We were going into town today. As of late we'd been avoiding town, at least Poppa'd been having me and Momma avoid town. The older boys still went whenever they had a need. Poppa didn't generally like going into town. He said there was too much opportunity to get into trouble.

I knew Poppa didn't like no kind of trouble. He was generally soft spoken and would walk away from confrontation. Although the only confrontation I ever saw him encounter was when Momma got mad. She rarely got mad these days, but if she did she went straight for the jugular. Poppa would tease her afterwards, when she got over it. He'd say she only had two modes, pure sweetness and pure meanness. He said that was the Indian side of her.

She didn't get physical at all but just said real mean things, saying she would divorce him outright and such. Divorce was a big taboo in those days; we kids would get real scared when we heard that. I couldn't imagine being able to face any of my friends again if'n Mommy and Poppa were divorced. Poppa would just walk away, he'd stay out of the house until Momma would call him to eat or find some other excuse to call him. We all knew then that Momma was over it.

This trip was to be one of those rare family trips into town. Poppa had a large section of timberland that his granpappy, as he called him, left him when he died. It was Indian deeded land. Poppa had just sold the rights to some of it to a timber company and gotten a check. Poppa said this was the first check he'd ever received in his life and showed it to all of us proudly.

Generally Poppa was a tinker and a trader. He'd fix all kind of things for people. Everything from time-pieces to automobiles. He also built barns and the like for people. Mostly, though, he was a trader.

He'd trade for anything of value. Once I remember him bringing home twenty to thirty long swords. He'd traded some farm equipment he'd just traded for the day before for them. Other jobs, like cutting timber, always paid cash.

Town wasn't but fifteen miles away, but I looked at it like it was going into another country. After Silas' dressing change was complete, Poppa went outside and sat in the flatbed truck. Momma and me wouldn't be ready for at least another half hour, that was expected, but Poppa would wait in the truck.

When Momma and me finally stepped outside, the three boys were already in the back of the truck. It was just a flat bed, with no sides at all. Del and Walt sat one on either side of Silas, leaning against the front cab. As Momma and me neared the cab, my three brothers made smart remarks about our tardiness.

"You boys just hush your mouths now, ya hear?" said Momma, and without waiting for a reply climbed into the cab and scooted next to Poppa. Climbing in next, I made it a point to give the boys as smug a look as I could muster. Poppa, always the peace keeper, didn't say a word, but he did have an impatient look on his face, and I thought he made it a point to shift into first a little noisier than usual. And off to town we went.

It was a warm sunny day, although humid. Which was starting to make me sweat. I secretly tried to lower my head so as I could smell my own armpit while my arm was up on the windowsill, the window being rolled down. I'd noticed lately that I was beginning to smell in my armpits when I sweat, something I'd never noticed before. The other day I'd made mention of it to Momma, she just said it was a part of growing up.

It wasn't hardly no time at all and the dusty old road had carried us into town. Poppa parked right in front of the town bank. There weren't no blacktop in town yet; it was all dirt and clapboard sidewalks.

"Wouldn't you know it?" said Poppa under his breath as he slapped the stick shift into park. "Those damn Lovett boys."

Just then a pot-bellied man strolled out of the bank, both hands in the front pockets of his overalls as he walked. Old man Lovett was jingling whatever change he had in his pockets every time I ever remember seeing him.

"Only a damn fool would tell the world he's got pockets full of change like that," Momma stated flatly. "Serve him right if'n he got robbed." Me and Momma giggled, putting our heads together.

Old man Lovett walked up to his three boys. They were standing right in front of the bank, making a pretense like they didn't even see us parked a few feet from them. The three boys were between the ages of sixteen and twenty. They were trouble, and their daddy, himself a loudmouth, seemed to egg them on whenever he could.

"Wait here, I'll just be a few minutes," said Poppa as he got out, more to the boys in the back than to me or Momma. As Poppa walked into the bank, the Lovetts walked off, looking as arrogant as four prize pigs toting first-place ribbons around their necks.

Old man Lovett was pot-bellied like a short-legged pig, but in denial. He walked with his legs swinging out wide from his body and his chest heaved up into his chin to give the impression his fat belly was really just an overgrowth of his massive chest. I don't think he succeeded in fooling anyone but himself.

After Poppa came out of the bank, he had a little bit more of a swagger himself. He proudly flipped two bits at me and then at Silas who caught it no problem with his bandaged hands.

"I'm a needin' some lumberyard supplies if'n you two want to run over to the food store and buy yourselves a little sweet each," said Daddy.

Momma started to say something but Daddy cut her off with, "We're meet you there directly. Then to Momma, "They're be all right Momma."

Cut loose, me and Silas jumped down from the truck and started walking fast to the food store just right across the street from the bank. As we got to the entrance, Silas got distracted by a stray dog out in front of the store which he stopped to pet. Without waiting for him I went on into the store and right up front to the counter.

This was the first time I'd ever been in a store by myself. Momma had always been with me before, but of recent I just hadn't been to town for quite some time. I walked right up to the counter and stood directly in front of the store-lady behind the counter and waited for her to address me like as Momma had told me was the polite way to be.

"I'm sorry, sweety, these nice folks were before you," said the kindly gray-haired lady behind the counter.

"Oh, that's fine, let her go ahead," stated the nice sounding lady of the elderly pair that I'd just inadvertently cut in front of. Besides them the store was empty of customers. Except for bulk items like the barrels that were in the middle of the floor, right next to the now not needed wood stove that would heat the store in the winter, everything else was behind the countertops.

Surrounding three sides of the store the counters separated the shelved kitchen and food items that lined the three walls from the customers. The store attendant acquired everything for the customers from those shelves.

"Ok, sweety, what can I do for you?" asked the smiling clerk.

"I'll take two of those peppermint sticks and two of the lemon sticks," I replied, trying to sound as lady-like as I could.

Just as she placed the four candy sticks on the counter and I'd placed my two bits on the counter in return, the door behind me opened and Silas walked in. Stopping in mid-reach for my payment, the lady behind the counter stopped and her pleasant demeanor soured.

"What do you want?" she demanded of Silas.

"Excuse me," she stated flatly, more to the elderly couple behind me than to myself. "We have to watch these little Indian kids like hawks, or they'll just steal us blind, they will," she said in explanation as she turned from us to get closer to Silas.

As she made her way around the counter separating herself from us customers, the elderly couple behind me suddenly noticed Silas' bandaged hands.

"Oh, look, both of his hands are all bandaged up," spoke up the woman sympathetically.

"Well, it's a known fact that these Indians don't take care of their kids. They just let them run wild throughout the countryside. That's how come they steal so bad. They just can't ever be trusted, at any age," stated her husband.

Standing there, at that time, I suddenly became acutely aware of the difference between mine and Silas' skin tones. I was fair, light hair and light brownish-green eyes. Silas was much darker compared to me, black hair and dark eyes as well.

"Here! Little boy," angrily asked the sales lady as she neared Silas. "What are you doing in here unsupervised?"

"He's my brother," I spoke up quickly.

I was suddenly the object of attention. The sales lady's mouth was plump open. I turned to the nice old couple behind me; they weren't smiling no more.

As the silence made no move to abate, I took up my two bits from the counter and started walking rather hurriedly toward Silas. As I took his arm and turned him towards the door, I heard the old man say, "Must be from one of them damn abominable mixed marriages.'

"A breed?" replied his wife with unfeigned sympathy in her voice.

I don't think the sales lady ever has closed her mouth.

Chapter 9

That next day found us walking the stretch to Uncle Bear's, me and my three brothers. Silas was talking up a thunderstorm, but me, I was feelin' mighty down. Although I didn't want to admit it I knew it was the store episode yesterday that was frettin' me.

The walk today seemed unbearably long and the heat of the morning didn't help none. When, finally, Uncle Bear's stone entryway pillars came into view marking his property line, the boys took off at a run. Me, I hung back. I wanted time to myself to think.

As I eventually strolled up to Uncle Bear's house, I could hear the boys off shooting back in the thicker woods behind Uncle Bear's home. Silas screamed excitedly. There was some clanging, metal on metal, coming from Uncle Bear's garage.

The garage was made of the same stone as the house, all gathered from right there on Uncle Bear's small patch of land. It had two bays; they were open faced, no doors of any kind. The garage was basically three walls and a roof.

As I entered one of the two bays, separated by a stone pillar that helped brace the roof, I saw Uncle Bear in the back, working on something. He smiled and waved as soon as he saw me.

Walking toward him, I passed by his various tools. Uncle

Bear chipped rock as much as anything else. If asked I really couldn't say what exactly he did. I knew he was well off, extremely rare for a half-breed Indian in those days. I'd heard mention once he was some sort of a war hero and had an income from that. Once I heard mention of him selling some rare artifact to some antiquities dealer and making a lot of money. I even heard him called a flint knapper once, but I didn't know what that meant.

I looked at all the strange objects now, stacks of gunnysacks and tin coffee cans lining one shelf. Giving in to curiosity I looked in one, just rusty nails sitting in water. There were tools of all sorts, metal, leather, things I never could have guessed what they'd be used for.

"The boys said you was mopin' around like a tick without a hound dog; what's frettin' you, girl?" asked Uncle Bear directly.

I planned on puttin' on airs like I didn't have a care in the world, but Uncle Bear knew how to get through such defenses. Without even sayin' hello I burst into a full account of the happenings of yesterday in town. I told him how ashamed of myself I was, because I didn't say anything to defend myself or Silas. How I hated my own white skin. Those store people had been prejudiced against Silas because he looked Indian. They'd only felt sorry for me because I wasn't all white like I looked.

Uncle Bear listened, giving me his full attention, looking down at the ground the whole time. I hadn't told Momma or Poppa what had happened yesterday, I was too ashamed. There was just something about Uncle Bear, you could tell him anything. When I finally finished Uncle Bear remained silent for a long instant. He was sitting on a wood stump, a chisel and hammer in hand, facing a large stone he'd been shapin' into something else.

"You know," Uncle Bear started slowly, "I was a young man when World War I started. I'd never been out of the state of Oklahoma when I signed up for the military. I told them I wanted to fly planes.

"It was a big deal at the time. No Indian had ever tried to sign up to fly planes before. At first I was flatly told no. But as I kept requesting that position, they finally allowed me to train to fly.

"After I became a pilot me and two other fellas were decorated for our deeds in combat, we saved a high-ranking dignitary's life. The other two pilots were white guys. They were given choice properties in states of their choosing. Me, I was given this little plot of land you're on right now.

"The first time I came here after the war, I could see why they wanted to get rid of it. It was one big rock pile. I'd been given a rock mound.

"I remember my brother Joe laughed and said, 'What did you expect, you crazy Indian, you thought the white government was a gonna give you somethin' worth havin'? This is the middle of nowhere.'

"And it was, too. No roads within twenty miles even, just a marked off lot in the most remote section of Indian Territory. At first I was deeply hurt, on the verge of being really bitter. After moping around for a week here, I told Joe, 'You go on home. I'm staying here, you say this is nowhere, I say I'm now-here.'

"He did leave and I stayed and built this house and garage and all the rock entryways with the rocks available. And I've been living off those same stones ever since."

I sat where I'd seated myself, next to the stone that Uncle Bear had been carving.

"You see, it was all in perspective—one man's nowhere was my now-here. I made the choice to quit feelin' sorry for myself, no matter my excuse, and to start from where I was.

"You can't hate part of who you are without hurting all of who you could become," said Uncle Bear gingerly.

"But life don't have to be so hard, do it?" I asked on the verge of tears.

Uncle Bear laughed like I'd said something hilarious, slappin' his bold spot with his palm.

"I guess it do, 'cause it is," he replied. "Each hardship we go through braces us for the next. But there's a lot of good mixed in there too.

"I guess if there's a secret to life it's to bare the hardships: relish the good times and laugh during it all so if'n there is a devil planning agin you, he won't be able to tell what happenings are oppressin' and which are benefittin you."

The rest of that day was spent in talking with Uncle Bear. We talked while he chipped on his stone. He was working on what looked like it would be a squatting figure of a man, about a foot and a half tall. The figure was holding a hatchet across his chest with one hand.

"I been wondering," I opened up. "How come you, Poppa and Momma showed up just in time that time at the barn fire?"

"That was your poppa's doin'," he responded with some thought behind it. "He and your Momma drove up kind of in a hurry and your poppa jumps out and yells, 'Where's the kids?' I knew then to be concerned myself.

"I felt it then, too," he stated, after a short pause. "I knew you three was in danger and you was at the old barn. I should've torn that thing down long ago," he stated sorrowfully, shaking his head.

"But how did *he* know?" I implored.

"He just knew," Uncle Bear stated after another pause. "You'll know things, too. Some would call it 'psychic.' I don't know the full meaning of that word but we feel things, things relating to our loved ones and them bein' in danger and all. It don't always work, but your poppa's pretty sensitive when it comes to you kids."

I wanted to inquire more, but I could hear my brothers a'comin'. I'd wait for another time. Silas ran straight up to me, looking feisty, and blurted out emphatically, "What ya' doing out here anyway for, girl? Don't cha' know a woman's place is in the kitchen? Me and my kin here's a hungerin'." His arms were flailing passionately in the direction of Del and Walt.

It didn't take me no time to rise and start the pursuit. Silas had been ready; he ran ahead of me, just out of arm's length. Once or twice I could have caught him, but that wasn't the point. After several minutes I got tired and meandered toward Uncle Bear's house. I'd cook then we'd walk home; this had turned out to be a great day.

By the time we finally headed home that evening, it was later than we usually left Uncle Bear's. We took our leave and started walkin' just as dusk was hintin' to set in.

Del and Walt had shot up all the ammo they'd brought so decided to leave their rifles at Uncle Bear's for the night, as we hoped to return tomorrow. They took the lead as me and Silas trailed behind, Silas talkin' a mile a minute about nothin'.

Dusk was a full reality by the time we were nearing the halfway point. The sound of an automobile clanging down the gravelly road behind us made me stop and look for safety's sake.

As the pick-up started to pass it slowed down and I could see ole man Lovett leering at me from behind the wheel. Two sons were sitting up front with him and the last son in the back with three others.

"Hey, *squaw!*" jeered Todd Lovett, the oldest, who was sitting at the passenger door.

"Hey, look," shouted Nat from the back of the truck, "it's that half-breed burned boy and his squaw sister."

As everyone laughed, the truck sped up again, throwing gravel in our direction. I grabbed Silas from behind and turned him so as to use myself as a shield to protect him. The smell of liquor seemed to linger behind the truck as it sped on.

Up ahead Del and Walt had heard something; they were too far up ahead to hear the exact words but as they stopped to look at the upcoming automobile their faces showed concern.

"It's ole man Lovett and his bastard boys," spat Walt.

"Yeah, well, we ain't had no trouble with them for a while, so they ain't got no call to bother us," replied Del as he and Walt edged to the side of the road.

The truck never slowed down as it sped past Del and Walt, but there were stern looks sizing up the two from all those within. When they were well past, one of the boys in the back of the truck flung a beer bottle in the two's general direction. It broke in the ditch that ran alongside the road, put there for drainage, a safe distance from Del and Walt.

"They's lookin' for trouble no doubt," said Walt. "I wish we had our guns and they was loaded."

"This ain't no shootin' matter, but it may turn into a fightin' matter," replied Del, his look intent on the road up ahead where the Lovett truck was turning around on the narrow dirt and gravel road.

As the two watched the returning truck slowly make its way back towards them, me and Silas made to speed up so's we could be by them, that much the safer.

We weren't quite caught up to where Del and Walt waited when the Lovetts made their way past again. They waited until they were closer to us than to my two brothers before they started to hurl insults this time.

"Half-breeds!"

"White squaw!"

Most of the insults were thrown at us because we were mixed, but the nastiest sounding insults were always aimed specifically at me. It was as if I should feel extra ashamed because I had the audacity to be light-skinned. I knew it was the remarks directed at me that got my three brothers the maddest also.

If I had been closer to Del and Walt, I'd have tried to minimize the damage by saying something to the effect that those type of people weren't worth worrying about what they said anyhow. But from where I stood I could see Del and Walt were fit to be tied they looked so mad. Even Silas threw back some choice phrases that I wouldn't have believed he was capable of.

Without a word I grabbed Silas by the arm and we started to run as the truck sped by us once again. By the time me and Silas reached Del and Walt, we could see the Lovett's truck was once again turning around.

"If'n we take off across this here field, we won't be bothered by them," I stated indicating our right.

"Like hell, I'll run from them Lovett bastards," snorted Walt. I could see he was hot under the collar now. I looked to Del to find some elderly intervention.

"That just won't do, little sis," Del stated resignedly. "If'n we got this to do then we better face up to it like men." He paused for a moment.

Del was a slow talker; every word that came out of his mouth was deliberate.

"If'n they's trouble," he turned to me, "you take Silas and skedaddle. Through this here field's a good plan. It'll save you a mile of walkin' on this here dusty road too," he added.

To Silas, "I know you ain't a'scared none, but you got to get sis here to safety."

The Lovett's truck was coming upon us now.

"You better get on now," said Del as he used my shoulder to guide me in the right direction. Me and Silas started walking, almost grudgingly. We went a short distance then stopped by an old oak tree. Grabbing Silas by the shoulders we disappeared behind it. I knew we couldn't get help in time, and I reasoned we could be there when the fight was over to help. Plus, the fact was, I wanted to see the Lovetts get their come-upons.

As the truck pulled to a stop just ahead of Del and Walt one tall, lanky boy jumped out from the back of the truck at Del. His intention had been to use the momentum from the jump to throw Del off balance and maybe even knock him over.

But as his feet touched down right in front of Del, Del grabbed both the boy's shoulders as his own knee jerked upward to find the boy's groin. Throwing the writhing form haphazardly off into the roadside ditch, Del braced himself for his next opponent. The unlucky youth never rejoined the brawl; from what I could see he seemed more interested in recuperating from what had just happened to him.

As the other three boys joined from the back of the truck and the two Lovett boys made to get out from the front cab, the fight was on in full force. One boy yielded a beer bottle and struck at Walt's head. He just barely ducked in time and responded with a hard-fisted uppercut that caught the boy squarely on the jaw.

The boy was stunned enough that Walt was able to redirect his attention just in time to brace himself as the youngest Lovett boy, Nat, barreled into his stomach in a low crouch. His intention having been to wrestle Walt to the ground, he got two crashing elbows in his back for his effort.

Del, in the meantime, took the last boy from the back of the truck toe to toe. I never learned that boy's name, but he was a fighter. Big boned, he was stout and obviously a farm boy; he was deep tanned and well muscled.

Both he and Del had drawn blood by the time old man Lovett's two older boys, Todd and Jesep, tried to join in. To the farm boy's credit he stepped back and stated flatly to the two, "This here's our fight. I don't want no hep from neither of ya' all." With that he rushed Del again, fists flailing.

Obviously this boy, probably about Del's own age of twenty-two, was something to be reckoned with because his words stopped the Lovett boys in their tracks. Almost instantly, however, they noted the boy Walt had stunned with his uppercut laying in the gravel road. Nat was crouched on all fours trying to catch his breath.

The two of them charged at Walt, who made an effort to sidestep the two downed boys and put the truck between himself and them to at least buy himself some thinkin' time. Getting an idea, I lowered my head to Silas, who I'd been holding close all this time, "Do you got your bean flip with you?"

Bandaged hands or no, I knew Silas was a darned good shot with his slingshot. Taking the "Y" shaped stick from his pocket, he reached into his front coverall pocket and produced several good sized throwin' stones.

As I let him go he stepped out from behind the large tree we'd been observing from behind and let his first stone go. Jesep had just started to approach Walt who was making his stand in front of the truck. This way Walt could also keep an eye on old man Lovett, who didn't seem inclined to participate, but Walt wasn't taking any chances.

Todd was going around the truck to approach Walt from behind. Just as Jesep made his move to rush Walt, a stone caught him cleanly behind the ear. Jerking away from the impact Todd threw himself into the open passenger door of the truck, bounced back and fell head over heels into the roadside ditch only a few feet away.

Unsure of what had just transpired, Walt turned his full attention on Todd, who hadn't hoped for as much. In the meantime, Nat, who'd been preoccupied in his recovery from the back blows, jumped to his feet and rushed Walt from behind.

Grabbing Walt around the waist once more, this time from behind, Nat half-swung Walt around, who was taken by complete surprise. The move turned out in Walt's favor, however, as just then Todd swung his large fist right at Walt's face. He missed, falling forward from his own momentum.

Recovering from the initial surprise, Walt countered with a hard right on Todd's cheek, dropping him to the ground. Nat still struggled to do something with Walt now that he had him in a solid grip from behind. Twisting to the right and left, Walt couldn't get free or turn around either one. Nat, however, couldn't do anything but hold on at this point. Walt just sidestepped every effort Nat made to throw him down.

Finally Nat stepped off the road into the deep ditch, and tumbled down, bringing Walt to a landing on top of him. Landing on a large rock Nat gasped and let his grip on Walt go. Walt stumbled out of the ditch just in time to see Todd getting to his knees.

Looking over at Del, Walt saw him and the farmer boy resorting to wrestling now, both bloody and looking exhausted.

On the dirt road back toward Uncle Bear's, an automobile was coming.

Old man Lovett, observing the oncoming vehicle in his rear view mirror, honked the truck horn. "Get in," he drawled angrily.

Guardedly, keeping a wary eye on Walt, the boys started to get in the truck. Walt, just glad they were going, didn't make a move to stop anyone. Lastly, the farmer boy and Del broke up. They'd both been too tired to inflict much more damage on each other, they'd just been in a stalemate hold. Standing up tall, they glared into each other's eyes one last time then farmer boy jumped in the back of the waiting truck and it jolted down the road.

Standing alongside the road, Del, torn and bloody of face and clothes, Walt, dusty and tired, me and Silas who'd just ran up to meet them looked on as the old pickup that'd been coming slowed slightly as it passed us. It was old man Pete Sag and one of his boys, about Walt's age.

Pete was a full blood Indian, but he was no friend of our pa's or ours. Giving us a stern look as he passed, he kept on going. We was glad for that much; we wouldn't have wanted to have been beholden to his likes anyhow.

Pete was a showboat, leastwise that's what Pa called him. Once at a stomp, or powwow some took to calling it, Poppa spoke up against something Pete was proposing and the majority of those there took Poppa's side. Pete took it personal, mostly cause Poppa was only a "half-breed." Pete prided himself, and told it frequently, that he was a "full-blood."

Since that time our chickens had been showing up missing or dead. We used to let them out at times from their coops as our dogs knew better than to kill them. Walt had tracked several tracks from these instances and they always led straight to the Sag's land that just happened to adjoin our own. We all referred to him as "chicken-Pete" because of this.

There was nothin' to do but start walkin', and that's what we did. By the time we reached home, Poppa had already "felt" something. He and Momma both were standing out in our front yard looking down the road toward our direction. As we approached, Momma saw the dried blood all over Del, screamed and started runnin' to meet us. Poppa's face went stern and I saw him cock the lever action on a 30/30 he'd been holdin'."

Del really wasn't bad hurt, but there was a lot of blood all over him. He and farmer boy both had been bleeding from the nose and several other cuts and scrapes before their scrap had been halted. Once cleaned up, he was just bruised and swollen, nothin' broken. Walt had his share of scrapes as well. Silas entertained us by tellin' us of his part in the fight. Mostly he acted out how he took Jesep out of the fight.

No amount of levity, however, was gonna simmer down Poppa; he wanted war. While Momma tended to Del and Walt at the kitchen table, Poppa was pacing back and forth. Every now and then he'd recheck one gun or another for bullets or cleanness, or who knows what. He had, probably, six to eight guns already loaded and laid out on the kitchen table. It was dark outside so he'd gathered several extra kerosene lamps to take along.

"Are the boys alright, Momma?" Poppa spoke for the first time.

"They'll be fine, they just need a little time to heal is all," replied Momma, starin' at all the guns on the table before her.

"Good, then quit yer dotin' over them and let us get to evenin' the score."

Momma was silent. She knew there was no bluff in Poppa once he set his mind to something. Momma looked thoughtful for a long instant then, sitting her feet apart she turned to Poppa and assumed an expression of pure resolve like I'd never seen the like of on her pretty face.

"Now you listen here, Poppa. There won't be no revenge war unless'n it's sanctioned by the women folk, and that there would be me and no one else. You claim you respect tradition to these here kids, then you better live up to its rules now.

"Ain't no war, no killin', no nothin' unless'n I says so. And that's not a decision to be made unless'n the suns up neither."

I'd never known Momma to use traditional beliefs to pull rank on Poppa before, but she did it this time, and it worked. Poppa moped around the house for a couple of days after that, carrying loaded weapons wherever he went, but Momma never sanctioned no war.

The boys recovered and Poppa started usin' this gallon-size bottle of Vaseline on Silas' hands. He'd rub the Vaseline gingerly into his hands and each individual finger would get massaged and caressed with the Vaseline. His hands weren't covered with dressings anymore. They looked horribly scarred and gnarled, but he didn't cry hardly much at all because of pain anymore.

Chapter 10

Two weeks had passed since the boys had fought with the Lovett bunch. Silas' hands were coming along great. He was getting some movement back in them. Poppa would flex each joint, rubbing generous amounts of Vaseline into them as he did each day.

Poppa'd been bein' gone a lot tinkerin' and tradin'. Even Uncle Bear was gone. Gone to California. I overheard Poppa tell Momma he was a gonna sell some, "ancient Inca relic" he'd dug up to some artifact dealers he knew of. Poppa laughed and Momma shushed him. I didn't understand what all that was about, and I wasn't meant to.

That morning, over breakfast, Poppa announced he had his "feelin'." We were all cautioned to be, "extra careful and not invite no trouble, if'n they was a route to high foot it the other direction." We knew Poppa was sensin' something that was a gonna happen to one of us. He couldn't predict the future but he had his senses, and they proven right more n' once.

Poppa was "goin' tradin'" and he "mightn't be back till late tonight," he announced. Walt was eager to go with him, but Del declined. I knew Del'd been secret footin' it around with a white girl. That could only spell trouble I reckoned. Walt knew too, but he wouldn't tell Momma or Poppa. We had an unspoken sense of juvenile camaraderie; it was like belonging to a secret club, where all adults were deemed "non-applicable."

After Poppa and Walt left and all the chores were done that needed doin' Del casually announced that he was a goin' to visit some friends. Momma didn't pry, but she did raise one eyebrow. The rest of what happened that night I've gleaned over the years.

Del and his good friend Wally Wildcat walked into the barn. "The barn" was just that, an old barn that was being used to substitute as a bar. It was in the middle of what used to be a large cornfield, built to be central to the harvest.

The owners long ago quit harvestin' corn and started "harvestin' lost souls instead," as one old local preacher put it one Sunday over the pulpit. It turned out that that was the biggest promotion the barn could have gotten, and now it was the most popular place around among the younger crowd.

It being fairly remote, at least outside of any township, there were no racial discriminatory lines. All heathens, no matter what the racial profile, could come freely and defile themselves liberally. This also assured all that there would be at least one fight a night, usually more.

Del and Wally nudged their way through the crowd and straddled the makeshift bar, thick, rough-cut planks of wood sitting on wooden barrels the length of one wall. Taking their poisons of choice, they next made their way to the back of the barn where they recognized some friends.

Wally was full blood Cherokee and Del was dark enough that he could have been. Anyway, Del had fought for his right to run with whoever he chose. Besides their friends gathered where they were there were also a few unfriendly faces, namely, the Sag boys. Del wasn't one to be bothered by others till they made it a point to bother. Him and Wally were soon laughing and talking with their friends.

They'd been preoccupied with getting drunk and just having

fun in general when Del turned and was surprised to find himself face to face with Farmer Boy from the fight two weeks ago. It was apparent that it hadn't been deliberate on Farmer Boy's part either as they both stood speechless initially.

Del regained his composure first. "Excuse me," he stated flatly, aware that everybody around knew their history, not wanting to give away anything that might be taken as fear, but not wanting any trouble either.

"Excuse me," Farmer Boy replied, emphasizing the *me*. His expression gave nothing away but he made it a point to walk around Del without bumping him and went his way. The Lovett boys and others followed, all sneering in Del's direction.

"He *respects* you," Wally said incredulously, slapping Del on the back.

Everybody that was around Del was nodding in agreement, and the thought came as a shock to Del. As he was absorbing that he just happened to look in Pete Sag junior's direction. For whatever reason it was apparent that Pete was furious, as he was castin' his worst evil-eye right in Del's direction.

For the next hour or so Del enjoyed several more beers and a few shots of some particularly vile brew that passed for the house whiskey. Suddenly Del was pulled from a mild stupor back into the noise and hubbub of The Barn. At least two fights were breaking out, one in the far corner and one not too far from where they now stood.

It was Wally who was doing the pulling, "Come on, let's get out of here, before we get into trouble."

Half walking and half being led by Wally, Del started his commute out of the tangle and maze of The Barn occupants. Their attempted exit took them right past the closer fight. Edging past the crowd, Del saw what looked like Farmer Boy and Pete Sag Jr. going blows.

"Boy is Pete going to get his ass kicked," Del thought.

Just as they were passing by, the crowd parted and Del saw two clenched bodies being catapulted his way. Del's reflexes were definitely impaired as he made a feeble effort to get out of the way in time.

Before his mind could fully register what was happening, he found himself under the struggling pair. As he instinctively struggled to get out from under the two, he realized Farmer Boy was directly on top of him and Pete was pushing down on the two of them. He was also aware of warm liquid that seemed to be flooding over him.

Pushing with renewed effort he was able to roll out from under the pair. Now, the roar of the crown returned to him with added emphasis as he realized women had started screaming unlike before; this was usually a marker that things were getting more serious.

Attempting to get up, on all fours now, Del looked to the left and saw the limp body of Farmer Boy just inches away, oozing blood from a gaping wound on his left side. Del also noted the murder weapon just inches away from his left hand. Rising to his knees Del realized he himself was covered in blood that was not his own.

One more glance and he saw Pete pushing his way through the shocked crowd, trying to leave the premises. Once again the familiar tug on his shoulder as Wally urged him to his feet and he and Del made a harried exit.

He felt himself being boosted into the cab of Wally's old truck. His mind spinning from the alcohol and the shock of what he just saw, Del leaned his head back on the seat and closed his eyes. He could hear the sound of the road being thrown past them as Wally gunned the hesitant motor and hurled them down the dirt road toward home.

Chapter 11

As Wally raced into the driveway, screeching to a halt, even though it was late, Poppa and Momma were both waiting up. Seeing the haste of the arrival and the slumped over figure of Del in the passenger seat, spurred by his own intuition, Poppa rushed out of the house, with Momma a close second.

Wally, foreseeing the impending crisis, hurried to get out of the truck and explain that Del was alright before his parents saw his blood-soaked garments. Too late, Poppa had the passenger side truck door open and Momma was screaming. Poppa made to start stripping Del's limp figure down to reveal the hidden wounds just as Wally edged around a now frantic Momma and spoke up quickly.

"He's all right, Mr. Twosinger. That's not his blood, he's just had a little too much to drink. He didn't get in a fight or nottin', he just got soaked by someone else's misfortune."

Then, as Del slowly started to arouse and Poppa and a near panicked Momma, could see he was all right the hectic scene started to mellow out. Of course, by this time, the whole house was awake, and as we all milled around, Poppa and Wally helped Del from the vehicle and ushered him into the house.

Once inside the house, Poppa and Wally took the staggering Del to his room upstairs. Stripping Del down completely, Poppa listened as Wally went over the events of the night. Momma stood in the doorway and listened, too; me and Silas were shooed back to our rooms. That night Poppa burned every shred of Del's blood-soaked clothes out in the back yard.

Early the next morning I was up earlier than usual. Poppa was sitting on the porch, a throw blanket draped across his knees as he sat on our porch rocker drinking coffee. Across the throw blanket were two large western style six shooters and leaning against the porch railing was a double-barreled shotgun. It didn't look like he'd slept last night.

On the board slat porch nearby lay Walt covered haphazardly with a handmade patch quilt. Within easy grasping range lay his lever action 30/30. I ran to the kitchen where Momma was where I expected to find her, cutting potatoes at the kitchen table. She merely glanced up as I started helping, taking a chair beside her. There was anticipation in the air, and I noticed, a lady's sized lever action .22 caliber rifle leaning against the table.

After several minutes of muted silence, Momma spoke up, only a little terse, "You run get yer rifle, girl. Make sure it's loaded too, you hear?"

"Yes, Momma." Whatever was in the air I felt it too. One thing was for certain, it weren't fear. I passed Del and Wally coming down the steps as I bolted past them going up.

"I'm sorry, Momma," Del said as he approached Momma in the kitchen.

"Me, too, Mrs. Twosinger," Wally added sincerely.

The loaded gun leaning against the table didn't escape their attentions.

"Now you two just hush," Momma said as she wiped her hands on her apron and kissed Del on the cheek. Del had to bend down so she could reach it. Wally got a pat on the shoulder.

"I didn't mean to bring trouble home, Momma," Del added.

"That's what families for," stated Momma plainly as she turned back to her potato peeling.

"Now you two run along to Poppa, he'll be on the porch out front," Momma said dismissively.

Picking a rifle from several that were in the living room for himself, Del handed Wally a World War I rifle that worked as the two made their way to the front porch. Just as they were walking out of the house, they saw Daddy and Walt looking out across their large front yard toward the dirt road coming from town. There was a convoy of about six vehicles coming our way. Sheriff Mill's police wagon was in the front.

"I didn't do nothin' wrong, Daddy," Del said apologetically. "If'n I need to go to the police station and straighten this out, I will. I never meant to bring trouble home."

"I'm sorry too, Mr. Twosinger," piped in Wally.

Poppa sat in his rocker, silent, watching the approaching vehicles. Finally he spoke up, "Do you remember Evrett, the colored boy, son of old Mat Furlong?"

"Yeah," replied Del shaking his head in recognition. "He was about my age."

"Well, two nights ago they found him strung up, hanged by the neck until dead," continued Poppa, almost absent-mindedly.

"Someone accused him of chasing some white girl's skirt. The good, solid, white citizens took it upon themselves to dish out justice."

There was another moment of silence as Sheriff Mills and his posse turned their way into our property.

"No, sir," Poppa continued. "You won't be goin' nowhere with no white sheriff and his deputies."

As the vehicles pulled up towards the house, Poppa stood up, holstering the two pistols that had been in his lap. The lever action sound of a shell going in its chamber heralded Momma's appearance from the side of the house, a strategic location.

Casually Poppa hoisted the double-barreled shotgun up from its leaning position against the porch railing. As he did so, the barrel rested easily across the rail. Poppa stood there, letting those barrels point directly at the car Sheriff Mills would be getting out of. This fact wasn't lost on Sheriff Mills neither as he got out of the lead vehicle.

"Now, now, Mr. Twosinger, there ain't no call to be goin' and pointin' no gun at nobody," Sheriff Mills drawled as he stood on solid ground.

From my vantage point up on the second story, head peeking out from a windowsill, rifle ready, I could see all the other passengers of the other cars getting out and taking strategic places beside their vehicles; they were all armed. There were about six men per vehicle. This weren't never meant to be no friendly visit; this was a posse.

I turned swiftly as I heard a sound behind me; it was Silas, totin' his own gun. As he knelt down beside me and rested his gun on the windowsill next to mine, he looked up at me. His impression implied he was determined to be there, but at the same time needed some kind of reassurance he was doing the right thing, the way a child needs. I winked, he smiled and we both turned our whole hearted attention back to the scene unfolding below us.

Looking from side to side, to assure himself he was in the majority, Sheriff Mills continued, "Now, you know yo' boy there has been implicated in the murder of a good Christian white boy, jes' last night. He'll be a'needin' to come on down to the po'lice station and answer some questions."

"Would those be the same questions you asked young Evrett Furlong?" Poppa asked, enjoying Sheriff Mills' obvious bristling at the question.

Ole man Lovett, who'd come in one of the other vehicles shouted, "Blanket asses! We got no need to ask yo' permission. Let's just take the damn half-breed mutt and be done here," he incited.

I couldn't see what happened directly below me on the porch, but me and Silas took that as our cue and we both sited in right on Mr. Lovett. This fact wasn't lost on him neither, as he quickly backtracked the step forward he'd taken, glaring up at us. There was dust anew coming down the dirt road that led towards our house.

"That be the federal marshals a'comin'," drawled Sheriff Mills. "They get here and see this here standoff, that'll make ya'all outlaws. Obstructin' justice, that's what this here is called.

"Why, that's the problem with you inbred trash, you gots no character. We good Christian folk teaches our chillins ta' obey the law and respect authority."

There were heads nodding in agreement all around Sheriff Mills; his tone was flat, not accosting. What he spoke wasn't meant to be insulting; in his mind he was just speaking the plain truth. He'd have been shocked at the thought that we found his comments derogatory. We were inferior to him, and he just assumed we accepted this fact as readily as he himself.

"Why it's no wonder yo' young'uns should grow up to be murderers and whores." He made it a point to look up towards my direction. "You refused to let them go away to be taught Christian values. Why, in my day I'd have fought wildcats for the opportunity to learn pure Christian values the way yo' kids had a chance to. Instead I had to walk barefoot six miles to and from school each way, rain, shine, snow or high water."

With this comment he took the time to reacquaint himself with those in his accompaniment, looking around. He got nods of affirmation from one and all.

"Yeah? I'll wager both ways was uphill too," spoke up Poppa harshly, breaking up the good ole boy's re-acquaintance moment. Poppa was mad now, I could hear it in his tone, fightin' mad. He'd have said more I think, but just then Uncle Bear was pulling into the drive leading up to our house.

Braking to a halt near Sheriff Mills' own vehicle, he stepped out. As he did so all eyes were upon him. His presence seemed to add a new dimension to the posse out in front of our house. His appearance was obviously not a welcome one to anyone accompanying Sheriff Mills.

Just as casually as you please, Uncle Bear raised what turned out to be a Tommy gun to his shoulder and stated loudly, "Well, well, I didn't know you had comp'ny," addressing Poppa . "Had I known I'd have come sooner." With this he faced Sheriff Mills squarely. "I've just come to do some target shootin' with my brother and his family here. So, what brings all you fine, upstandin' citizens a callin'?" Uncle Bear spoke just as friendly as if he was addressing a church social.

There was no warm greeting in reply though, so Uncle Bear continued, addressing Poppa, "Well, brother, seen any varmints about that we can set in our sights?"

Slowly, casually, Poppa looked over the group of men in front of our house. "I've seen a few," he finally stated pointedly.

With this Sheriff Mills snorted in disgust, "You listen here, you damn breed, we'll be back. You all will have to answer to the po'lice for this here obstruction of justice." And he proceeded to get back in his police automobile.

Others of the gang also started re-attaching themselves to their vehicle seats, each showing their disgust for this change of events in their own way.

"Blanket asses!"

"Worse than the damn jiggaboos; at least they know their place."

From my vantage point, I saw Mr. Lovett getting back into the ride he'd rode in with. As he did so, he unobtrusively threw a rope into the floorboard, a hangman's noose on one end. And just as quickly as they'd drove up they were trailin' down the dirt road away from our house.

Chapter 12

I swatted at the fly that kept trying to make a landing on my nose. It was a nice, cool evening and there were lots of stars out. I was hunkered down behind the woodpile that lay between our cornfield that ran parallel to our house and our house itself.

I wasn't looking too mighty hard at the stars this night, though. My sights were set steadfastly toward the cornfield. My sights were literally set toward the cornfield as I gripped Poppa's 410 shotgun, barrel resting across the woodpile I crouched behind. Next to me was Silas, he with his own .22 caliber armament.

"I heard something!" he blurted out urgently, for about the twelfth time in the last half-hour.

"Sshhh! That was *me*, same as last time." I scolded.

It had been two days since Sheriff Mills and his "posse" were sent away from our house. After that Uncle Bear had been filled in on what it had all been about.

"If you didn't know what was a goin' on, how come you was to show up just in the nick of time?" inquired Silas, something I wanted an answer for, too.

"Well, your Poppa ain't the only one that gets his 'feelin's,'" Uncle Bear had replied.

Later that night, as I eavesdropped from the top of the

stairwell, I heard Uncle Bear telling Momma, Poppa and my older brothers that he had to go away for a week or so. He had some kind of business deal to make with some big-shot museum people back East. Something about some Inca artifacts he'd dug up down Mexico way. Uncle Bear, Poppa and the boys all laughed but Momma didn't.

"And what if'n yo' artifacts be proven fake? What then?" asked Momma in her rebuttal voice.

"They've been tested before, and always proven to be 'genuine,'" Uncle Bear replied, and the menfolk all laughed some more.

The talk had went into the night, but I'd snuck back to my room, exhausted from all the excitement of the day. The next morning, early, I'd barely gotten up in time to see Uncle Bear off. Running out in my nightgown, I ran up to the car window to wish Uncle Bear a safe journey.

"Don't you worry none now, you hear, girl?" he'd reassured.

"When will you be back?"

"I should make my deal and return within a week."

As he drove away, I saw the figure he'd been carving the day I'd been out at his place sitting in the back seat.

Later that day some friends of Poppa's had come by. The whole town was talking about how he and Uncle Bear had stood down Sheriff Mills and all those other "fine upstandin' white town folk." Apparently it tarnished Sheriff Mills respectability and chafed his pride to boot.

Poppa's friends warned him that folks were angry, what with the murder of a white boy and all. There was some talk that Del wasn't the murderer at all; several witnesses told Sheriff Mills so, that it was that Sag boy. But no matter now, the God fearin' population were worked up and itchin' for a hangin'. The Sag boy was nowhere to be found, and what with Poppa having backed all those white folk down, there was a lot of injured pride to be saved.

It was later that evening that specific plans had come to us.

Matt Sanford looked like a white man but he was really only half. Light skin, sandy hair and bluish eyes. He was married to an Anglo woman and lived in town. His real last name, before he changed it to fit into the main society more, was Searches Far. It wasn't too uncommon a practice, to alter one's Native name to fit in better.

Being accepted as a regular town's person he was privy to all the town gossip. He had been living as an Anglo person to the extent that few people even knew he wasn't full white. He even went to church at the church in the middle of town. All other Natives were confined to the Indian Mission outside of town if they chose Christianity for their faith.

Matt, however, still held loyalties to his Indian ancestry. Once Poppa had spent nigh all night pulling Matt, his wife, and kids out of a flooding road. Then he'd put Matt and his family up at our place overnight. They were all covered with mud and we'd dug up clothes that fit them all and they'd cleaned up and ate at our place. The next day the flood abated and they'd taken their leave, but Matt wasn't one to forget a favor.

"You best stay on yo' toes," he told Poppa, while I eavesdropped around the corner of the house. He and Poppa were talking out in the front yard.

"I don't know the specifics, but folks are almighty mad at what you done. They're talking about it like you stood at the cross of Jesus and belittled *Him*. Sheriff Mills is madder than if you'd slapped his momma and groped his wife.

"They're planning something and my guess is it'll take place at night."

Poppa had thanked him. That night we'd stood guard, just like we was a doin' now. Nothin' had happened. The next day, while I caught up on my sleep, Poppa had been buildin'. He took our old flat bed truck and turned it into a hotel.

Building up sides made of wood and stickin' a roof on top, we had room for sleepin' and out of the weather both. Momma had been boxing canned goods, and Walt and Del was loading essentials into the newly made camper.

"Are we goin' somewhere?" asked Silas excitedly.

"Can't say jest yet," Poppa replied. "But it pays to be ready jest in case." With that he ruffled Silas' hair and gave me a wink.

With what was left of that day everybody was instructed to pack our bags with clothes and needed items and these were placed in the back of the truck also. Now night wasn't too far off, and here Silas and I were, though we were both a'scared, Silas more than me, we were also excited. We sensed something was on the horizon.

We'd been livin' where we were now for all my life. We were here on family Indian deed land. That meant that, although as a tribe we'd been given much more land, when the government wanted to take most of it away, legally, they changed the rules.

Now, instead of a tribe with a large portion of land, we had individual families with small portions of land. Not surprisingly, all the surplus not given out per strict regulations went back to the government. This had been done under the pretext of "teaching the Indian self reliance and self determination through their gradual assimilation into the general populace."

Poppa said it was the Wyandotte Nation that deeded the whole of Ohio to the U.S. government, so we were used to such "assimilation" that always seemed to be to our detriment. Once Sheriff Mills, at the town meeting, had made mention of the fact that since the U.S. government had fought and defeated the Indians then we should be thankful that we wasn't just stripped of all our rights, like history shows other peoples have been by *their* conquerors.

Poppa had taken the platform, having been an open forum, and brought up the Treaty of Greenville and how way back the American government had acknowledged the Native American's right to what had been theirs for long before the first non-Native had stepped on this soil.

Also, in writing, the governmental officials swore to deal

with Native Americans as self-governed, lawfully and justly. When Poppa said we, as a people, weren't a defeated nation but rather were besieged and deceived, the assembled non-Natives were looking for a rope. There'd been enough Natives on hand that he'd been able to make a hasty retreat. But Poppa was pretty much scorned by the townspeople after that.

Chapter 13

Voices, there were definitely voices coming closer through our corn field. Thinking quickly I slapped my hand over Silas' mouth who was about to say he heard voices. With my index finger in front of my mouth to signal "hush" I retracted my hand and slowly cocked my rifle.

"Don't you go shootin' unless'n I shoot first, you hear?" I warned Silas as he steadied his rifle on the woodpile and found his sights. He nodded, wide-eyed. Off to our left there were several shots.

There was movement directly in front of us in the tall standin' cornfield. Me and Silas watched anxiously as corn stalks swayed from side to side as whatever was approaching made its way ever closer. Whatever, or whoever, was making their way toward our house was not a lone entity. From the amount of swaying corn it looked like there was a good number a'comin'.

"Okay, Silas," I turned to him anxiously now. "If'n you see someone you know don't belong here you just shoot, okay?"

Silas nodded. I wanted off the hook. I didn't think I'd have the gumption to order the shootin' of someone else, either by word or deed.

Poppa had always said, "Courage wasn't a matter of being able to look fear in the eye, but rather to look away from fear long enough to do what needed doin'."

Well, fear was starin' me flat in the face now and I wasn't sure I could look away. I cleared my throat. Silas looked over at me and I tried to give him a reassuring nod, only I don't think my head ever really moved. Seeing someone start to emerge from the cornfield our attention was riveted back to the situation at hand.

Before I could have time to think, Silas squeezed off two shots, fast. The intruder, just starting to emerge and watching the house too closely, dropped with a thud and a moan back into the cornfield. We watched as he was apparently pulled back out of sight deeper into the field. There was a volley of return fire, all directed at the house; they didn't know where we really were.

Now there were corn stalks swaying to the right of our woodpile. The culprits probably thought to work their way to the back of the house more. I thought I could barely see the outline of a person through the stalks. Setting my sight, I was startled when I squeezed the trigger.

There were corn stalks torn from the impact as the rock salt that Poppa'd loaded this particular shotgun with tore its way toward its unlucky victim. The resultant yelp of a man in startled agony told me that a sufficient amount of my charge reached flesh.

Now there were volleys going off from the other side of the house. Silas was looking at me, scared.

"It's all right, you did good," I comforted. "Those men were coming to hang Del, now you wouldn't want that would you?"

Silas shook his head vigorously.

"Then keep your eyes open and don't be a'scared to shoot again," I admonished.

Waiting in silence we watched. It appeared that our adversaries from the corn patch had rethought their attack policy. After the rock salt had embedded in the last man shot, they just seemed to melt away. It seemed a long time but it probably wasn't when we heard a familiar voice. It was Walt.

"Sis, it's me, so don't do anything stupid, like shoot me."

We turned as he appeared from the side of the house.

"It's okay, they all left, I reckon."

That was all Silas needed to hear, he abandoned his weapon and high tailed it to find his momma.

"Nobody's been hurt," Walt told. "Did either of you have to shoot?" Walt asked.

"Uh, huh," I managed, waggin' my head like I was stupid or something. I managed to point toward the cornfield.

"You go on inside, I better check out the field," he said gingerly, and I ran.

About an hour later Poppa, Del and Walt came into the house. Momma, me and Silas were all cuddled up on the divan, like it was freezin', but it was actually pretty warm out. Silas was sound asleep against Momma on one side and I was holdin' on tight to Momma on the other.

"Well, we put lead into several of their carcasses anyway," Walt said as he came in.

"Ain't no call to say anything more about it," Poppa replied sternly. "We done what needed doin', nothin' else."

"All we done was to give Sheriff Mills more of an excuse to come agin' the whole family," Del said guiltily.

"We done what needin' doin', nothin' else," Poppa reinforced.

"Well," Del continued as he leaned his rifle against the wall in the closet, "I think I shoulda' jest turned myself in. Hell, I didn't kill that white boy, and they probably know it."

"This ain't no knowin' matter. It's a race agin' race matter, pure and simple. Guilty or no, Sheriff Mills would find some excuse to take you away from yo' Momma and me one way or another.

"This here fight started years ago when I first stood up to Sheriff Mills for sending Indian kids away to boardin' schools. There were schools right here, but they wanted to 'rescue' the Indian kids from growin' up as savages. So they figured to isolate them and send them away to be mistreated by all those 'fine' upstandin' white, Christian, do gooders.

"I wouldn't let them take any of you then and I won't let 'em now."

"But," Del persisted, "it was you always said a man should stand up for hisself."

"There ain't nobody goin' home with lead in their asses today that'll claim you didn't stand up for yourself, or anyone else in this here family for that matter," said Poppa resolvedly.

For the next hour or so we waited. We jumped at every sound outside, and we waited. We were under no illusions as to how seriously Sheriff Mills would take our latest reaction. He might not have officially been behind today's attempted raid, but we knew he'd been privy to it.

And now, with gun holes in some fine upstandin' citizens, lynch mob though they were, he'd have all the excuse he'd need to come a'stormin' over and take us all, one way or another. We got one more visit that day, from Matt Sanford this time.

"Sheriff Mills is deputizing every man with a gun that he can round up. He's sayin' ya'all opened fire on an unarmed town assembly that had come solely to peaceably request you give Delvin up to the proper authorities."

"That ain't so," explained Poppa. "Why, they come sneakin' through under cover. I yelled and gave them warning shots, but they kept a'comin'. We didn't open fire till they fired on us first."

"I believe you, and I read the sign just up the road. I stopped where a large number of automobiles had parked and a whole fistful of men had gotten out, milled around, like they was scheming. Some of them headed through the brush this way. They was armed too, lots of impressions of rifles butts on the ground from men leanin' on 'em and puttin' 'em down.

"But we both know, if'n this here goes through to Sheriff Mills likin', you and your whole family will take the fall. I'm jest speakin' as a friend."

"I know you are," replied Poppa reflectively. "When do you think they'll strike?"

"I don't rightly know. In fact, I believe, they're makin' it a point to exclude me from all the official plannin'. My guess would be they're either strike tonight, just after dark, or early tomorrow morning."

"Thanks, Matt, I know you're risking a lot by doin' this fer me," I remember Poppa had said, and they shook hands. During that exchange, Poppa had handed Matt a piece of paper, insisting he take it.

That was the last time we ever saw Matt Sanford. Years later we did hear he'd been ostracized in town and lost his job and his church title of deacon. Turned out him and his family had had no place left to go but to our old place. That piece of paper Poppa had handed him had been the deed to our house and property there in Oklahoma.

It wasn't much time after that that Silas, who'd been looking out the kitchen window all afternoon, shouted a warning.

"I see somethin' movin', I think I see somethin' moving out by the barn."

I ran to Momma and Poppa. Del and Walt ran for their guns. Poppa directed Del and Walt out the front door while he went headfirst into danger out the back door as the barn was facing the backside of our house.

Within a few minutes they'd rounded up the culprit, and Del and Walt were half carrying half dragging a big ole white boy into our kitchen. He'd been bleedin' some as evidenced by his blood-soaked clothing and having been brought into the house had apparently reopened whatever wound he'd incurred.

Placing him on the living room divan, Momma had a look-see at his wound while Poppa kept his rifle handy and Del and Walt stood by. He'd been shot low on the left side just above his hipbone by a small caliber gun.

"He's mine!" Silas exclaimed excitedly when he came into the room. "I shot him! Remember, sis? He was the one I shot coming through the cornfield trying to sneak up on the back of the house."

Sure enough, it made sense, after having been shot initially, he'd been dragged out of sight by his buddy. Then my rock salt had bit into flesh and he'd been abandoned. Apparently his first inclination had been to seek shelter as he'd made his way to our barn and hidden himself there until it seemed a little safer to make his way home. Only thing was, he was hurt worse than he'd known and had lost a lot of blood.

It turned out his name was Derg. He was from one county over and didn't know us personally; he'd just been invited to participate in a "half-breed lynchin'" and ended up shot in our living room being cared for by Momma.

"He needs a doctor," Momma finally said.

Poppa had been pacin' back and forth all evening since the shootin' and subsequent capture of Derg, and now, suddenly, he stopped.

"He needs a doctor and we need a way past Sheriff Mills," said Poppa, thinkin' out loud.

"Reckon we can trade, him fer me?" asked Del.

"No, no," replied Poppa. "I wouldn't trust Sheriff Mills word any sooner'n' I'd trust a banker named Judas.

"But just maybe, we can work something out," Poppa said.

Chapter 14

Taking all the worldly possessions that we were able to carry in our flatbed truck, we pulled out of our driveway for the last time. Me and Silas, we were seated up front, one on each side of Momma, clingin' onto her. I was trying not to cry; Silas was crying. Poppa was driving and Del and Walt were in the back, enclosed part, with our prisoner who was too weak from blood loss to pose any danger to anyone.

We were wary driving towards town, and loaded for bear. Up in the front seat there was a handgun for each of us and a few extra just in case. In the back Del and Walt had a full arsenal, loaded and within easy grasp. It was dark now, a very black night.

As we neared town, Poppa slowed down some, and boy, was he alert. We'd originally thought we might hit some roadblocks, but the going was clear, up into town. Poppa was pretty sure though that our house had been being watched. If we'd have gone another way but into town we'd probably been set on pretty fast. Poppa had said we needed to buy ourselves some time.

As we entered town, Poppa really got vigilant. He was craning his neck like a stud stallion lookin' over a fence at a mare farm. Much to his relief, and surprise, we pulled right up to the po'lice station without being accosted or hailed by anyone.

Poppa jumped out quick and braced himself. He had on his

double pistols and took a double barreled shotgun from behind the seat. Me, Momma and Silas weren't stayin' in no truck to watch. We were armed and up on the rough plank sidewalk in front of the sheriff's office just as quick as we could shuffle out of the cab. Walt joined us with a 30/30 and two or three pistols shoved down in his britches.

I'll never forget the look on Sheriff Mills' face as Poppa, Momma, me and Silas entered his office, uninvited, while Walt guarded the door and our truck from the outside. I think his initial instinct had been to reach for his gun but the look of two twelve gauge barrels starin' straight at a man has changed more 'n one initial instinct I'd wager.

"Delvin Twosinger never killed no boy," Poppa spoke firm. "But I knows if'n we wants to continue livin' here, and we does, then we needs to make things right with the law."

Sheriff Mills, still preoccupied with the unwavering stare of Poppa's twin barrels pointed directly at him, only nodded as he sat very still, hands resting on his desk where only minutes before he'd been eating his dinner.

"But, more 'n that, Delvin's been shot, low on the left side, and he's lost a lot of blood. Momma here has stopped the bleedin', but he needs a doctor. Now I know, if'n we took him to the doctor you'd just have him into jail here, so we brung him straight here.

"I want your word that you'll fetch him a doc right quick, jest as soon as we leave. I know if'n any of us stay the chances of trouble will go up, what with hard feelin's over today's incident out at our place and all, and I got my other young'uns to worry about." Poppa nodded toward Silas and me.

"I also want your word you won't let no lynchin' take place. I'd take that mighty personal." With that Poppa kind of wagged his shotgun up and down for emphasis.

By now Sheriff Mills was seeing he wasn't to be dry-gulched by Poppa and he tried hard to regain his composure.

"Well, that there is the first smart move I knowed you to do since this whole affair started."

"Then I have your word if'n we leave Delvin here with you, he will get a doc's attention right off? And you won't give him over to be lynched?"

"I'm a man of the law, and a man of my word."

Before Sheriff Mills could go into a spill about how his word was his bond or something of the sort, there was a sharp rap at the door. Momma opened the door cautiously, gun at the ready. It was Walt, and he'd been joined by many armed town folk. Apparently they'd been sent home to eat and arm and were to meet Sheriff Mills back at his office, more 'n likely for a midnight raid on our place.

"Okay, you go out there and tell them to back away from our truck so's we can safely bring Delvin in. We'll put him in a cell ourselves. Now, you know I'll shoot whoever needs shootin'," warned Poppa.

It was obvious that Sheriff Mills didn't like bein' at the end of Poppa's gun barrels, but he also had no doubts about Poppa's sincerity to shoot. I suppose he figured he could always get even with our whole family just as soon as he had Del in custody. The mob outside consisted of some thirty or so armed men, all angry. But Sheriff Mills went out in front of Poppa and got them to back a ways back from our truck, explaining what was taking place. We also encouraged them with our barrels pointing in their direction.

Poppa and Walt got in the back of the truck while me, Momma and Silas stood our ground. When they brought "Del" out, he was covered with a blanket and practically being carried by Poppa and Walt.

"Has his momma protectin' him, and his squaw sister. Only good for poon-tang anyhow."

As I remember it, many of the racial comments seemed to fall on me. I guess that was to enrage Poppa more and I could tell it hurt him, but he wasn't out to be manipulated.

Once we got Del safely tucked away in a cell, we made our

way back into our truck. Sheriff Mills made a pretense at keepin' the peace, but as we pulled out there were beer bottles breaking against Poppa's wooden frame enclosure on the truck.

Poppa headed straight out of town. We didn't know if'n they'd chase us or not, but we were committed to putting as much distance betwixt us and those town folk as we could, and as quick as we could.

We'd meet up with Uncle Bear somewhere between where we now were and our destination. Uncle Bear was apologetic for having not been there when we needed him the most, but we understood when he shared a wad of cash with us from his sale of the "rare Inca artifact" he'd "found." It was "startin' over money" for us, he explained.

We all wanted him to continue on with us, but he said he had his home already, "and weren't no one gonna get him off'n it." Poppa and him had planned this rendezvous at their last meeting I learned. I didn't know where we was headed yet, but I was caught up in the excitement of the road.

"Ain't no one's fault," Uncle Bear told Del. "Just time to move on. Life's an adventure, don't ever be afraid of a change."

The Twosinger family continued on our way, "to Arizona," is all me and Silas could get out of Poppa. Sitting up front in the cab still with Poppa, Momma and Silas I looked down at Silas' hands. The scars were abating. Poppa still spent each evening rubbing Vaseline into Silas' hands, massaging and flexing. Years later there wouldn't be a single scar, no indication whatever, that a doctor had had reason to tell Momma Silas would never use his hands again.

We'd hear later, from Uncle Bear, of how furious Sheriff Mills was the next morning when he finally had the doctor over to view "Del" in his cell. Poppa had figured right that Sheriff Mills wouldn't go and fetch the doc till the next morning. It was just his way of showing how little he thought of us "breeds." The ploy had bought us all the time we needed to get out of Oklahoma though.

Chapter 15

Our passenger side front tire was smoking like a chimney in wintertime as we pulled off the road toward a little clearing alongside Oak Creek. Poppa slowed the tiring truck down and came to a jerking halt not far from the remote riverside. As we all jumped out, eager to stretch our legs, Poppa made the prognosis.

"Well, it looks like the bearings done run plump dry." He stopped and thought a bit, staring down at the tire.

"I don't have any wheel grease but I could lubricate it real heavy with Silas' Vaseline, and it would get us into town. There's supposed to be a little town jest up a ways by the name of Sedona.

"Me and the boys could make it there afore dark if'n we hurried…"

"Oh, poo," interrupted Momma. "It can wait till tomorrow." Then, turning to me, "Girl, you go fetch the fixin's for some sandwiches."

As remote as our site looked, there were actually two other vehicles pulled off the road and parked as we were, near the creek shore. Just up the way was a dilapidated looking old car, and back the way we'd just come was an old pick-up that looked like it had hard won every mile it must have had on it.

As me and Momma fixed the sandwiches, we started to notice some Indian kids around me and Silas' own ages and several younger peering through the brush and trees that separated us from the vehicle up ahead of us.

"Looks like we got comp'ny," Poppa pointed out.

We'd made up more sandwiches than there were of us and Momma handed me and Silas several extras apiece. "Might as well be neighborly; go see if'n those kids is hungry."

Taking the extra sandwiches, me and Silas bashfully made our way toward the other kids. The younger kids took off like scared rabbits back towards their parents, who were sitting at the edge of the water. But the two kids about me and Silas' age stood firm.

They gladly took the sandwiches, and in repayment, seemed eager to show us something. We trekked past our own encampment, keeping a safe distance away per our new companion's promptings, and secreted over nearer the encampment below us. Peering over a dead tree from long ago the girl pointed.

"Dark."

Peering over cautiously it took me and Silas a few seconds to figure out what we were being directed at to see. Then it occurred to me, this was the first time these Indian kids had ever seen colored people.

"Colored folk," I said.

"Colored?" repeated the girl and explained further in a language I'd never heard the like of to her younger brother who seemed fascinated by the concept.

From what I could see of the colored family, there were a dad, mom and six kids, the oldest two not much different in age than us four. Me, Silas and our two new Indian friends snuck away and the rest of that day hung around together, playing in the water and getting to know each other.

It turned out they were Navajos, and except for Marybaa, the girl my age and Henry the boy Silas' age, none of the others spoke much English. The father knew some and seemed to understand, but the mom and younger kids were pretty much Navajo speaking only. They were all friendly though and seemed to be glad Marybaa and Henry had made friends.

It took some coaxing before Marybaa and Henry got up the gumption to meet our family. Finally, shy as they were, they allowed a formal introduction service to take place. Everybody gave their greetings and we went back to our creek-side playing.

Henry was fascinated by Poppa, who still wore his two six-shooters at his hips and Del and Walt, who were also visibly armed. Apparently they didn't have but one old gun that their daddy used for huntin' jack rabbits and prairie dogs with. Me and Silas laughed; we'd never heard tell of a prairie dog but we weren't into eatin' dog anyhow.

It was later when Marybaa finally asked me how come I was riding with those "other Indians" and where *my* daddy and mommy were, and also, if Del was one of us or from the colored family across the way. At first I was hurt that my new friend was no different than all those color-bound town folk back where we come from. But as I looked in her eyes preparing a torrent of rebuke to inflict in retaliation, I couldn't help but see nothin' but the purest curiosity. There was no hint of prejudice or dislike, just unknowin'.

Swallowing my defensive lump I simply explained, "We're all one family. Only we Wyandottes, we come in all shades. Daddy says like a herd of wild horses, some's solid colored, some got spots, somes light, somes dark. They're all horses."

Marybaa and Henry thought for a moment then nodded in understanding, and that was all there was to it. We played that evening away in the cool waters of our creek until we were called to supper by Momma. We encouraged Marybaa and Henry to come eat at our camp and when they did we were all surprised to see the whole Yazzie family already at our camp. Poppa and Momma had went and introduced themselves earlier and invited all to come eat.

By the next evening meal, me and Silas had gained another set of friends. The colored kids downstream of us were friendly and had finally come over and introduced themselves as we and our Navajo friends all played in the stream. Initially there'd been curious questions and introductions. But soon all differences seemed trivial as the sun was hot, the water was cool and we had a lot of energy.

That evening meal found three distinct families eating together—separated by races but all had similar human experiences. As the eatin' was done and all us kids took to playing away from the grown-ups, I snuck back and listened in to some of the grown-up conversation as was my long standin' habit.

Hue, the colored poppa, was telling the other grown-ups about how their oldest boy had been a victim of a white lynchin' back in Georgia. The boy, he said, had been Del's age. He went on to say how he'd just buried his boy and packed up all the worldly possessions the family could carry in their ole truck and headed West. Next thing he knew his truck was used up and here they sat.

I was drawn back into the tag team by a touch from Marybaa just then and was up and running to get rid of "it" just as soon as possible by touching someone else. It was close to dark when we herd of kids finally trickled back up to the campfire. It wasn't cold but I think it was the effect that prompted the campfire's existence.

Just as I approached the setting where all the grown-ups were sitting around Poppa arose with a hand to his gun. Then I saw Hue stand, coming up and gripping an axe by its handle that had been nearby in one motion. Then all the men stood and turned in the direction that was drawin' Poppa's and Hue's attention.

There, just appearing from around the heavy roadside brush, stood a white man. His gait showed obvious hesitation as he slowly approached our campsite. He timidly hailed the now upright gathering as he approached.

"Hello...the camp. Me and my family ran into some trouble down the road a piece. We...we hit a deer in the road," he said and laughed timidly, makin' it a point to keep his hands in plain site.

"There weren't no cure, we jest had ta' push the wreck to the side of the road best we could and start walkin'. I wouldn't disturb you folk, but fer the missus and the little 'uns, they ain't et today."

As he spoke there was a frail little woman holding a baby followed by three little kids, all stair steppin' down from little to littler come around the brush behind the man. The man himself looked like he was fairly starved with dirty, heavily patched but still torn, clothing. The woman and kids all looked like they was wearin' hand-me-downs that had been handed down one too many times. She stayed where she was when she saw her man facing what must have looked like a fairly hostile camp.

"Well, we'll jest go on up the crik a bit and bed down fer the night," he said as he started to back step, makin' it a point not to make any sudden moves.

He was halfway back to the road from where he'd stood and was still walkin' backwards when Momma finally spoke up.

"Nonsense," she said as she started up from the stump she was sitting on. "We got food a'plenty and won't turn no hungry folk away."

"You men folk," she said, turning to all those around the campfire in a tone that left no room for questions. "Make room for these folk while I get some food made up."

That camp out ended up lasting the whole of what was left of that summer. Our four families stayed right there beside Oak Creek, and we shared all that we had with them and they too shared what little they had. The summer, of course, eventually ended and we all went our separate ways.

What's important, Poppa said, was that we all parted friends and skin colors were all forgotten by the time we said our goodbyes. That truly was a summer to remember. We didn't solve no world problems, but we sure did have a colorful camp out.